Overture

by

Claire Davon

Lyrical Interludes, Book 2

Overture

Cover Art by *Kim Mendoza*

The Wild Rose Press, Inc.
PO Box 708
Adams Basin, NY 14410-0708
Visit us at www.thewildrosepress.com

Publishing History
First Edition, 2022
Trade Paperback ISBN 978-1-5092-4225-2
Digital ISBN 978-1-5092-4226-9

Lyrical Interludes, Book 2
Published in the United States of America

If he had been on fire before, now a full-on conflagration rushed through him. His body surged at the sensation of her curves. Her breath rushed out, warm and cold at the same time. Her lips were so close. He needed only to shift forward minutely to be kissing her. He peered into her eyes. Awareness flared in them as well. She smelled of snow—and woman. In her gaze was the promise of home and family. All the things he hadn't expected to find in Los Angeles.

He wanted to kiss her. He had to kiss her. Just as he was closing the distance, she made a low sound and backed away. He released her, trying to be glad that it hadn't happened. It would commit him to something he wasn't prepared for. He couldn't see what good could come out of being with her, yet he craved it like fire.

"I guess I am getting cold."

He sighed, trying to control his reaction. The time was lost. He should be grateful he hadn't done something stupid.

He longed for the missed opportunity.

"Can't have you catching your death. Let's get back in that car of yours and put on the heat. Then you can take me farther up into these mountains. Unless you need chains?"

She shook her head.

He should be grateful they hadn't breached the gap. Once they did, there would be no going back.

He told himself that's what he was feeling. Gratitude.

Sure, he was.

Acknowledgments

The first version of this book was written over a decade ago. At that time, it was not connected to the book that eventually became *Reprise*—that happened later. I like to think that it was always in the back of my mind, waiting to be noticed.

Thank you to Debbie, Paula, Gil, and Robin for enjoying what is now *Overture*. I hope this revised story delights you every bit as much as the early draft did.

I would also be remiss if I didn't extend my most grateful thanks to Josette, my amazing editor. Thank you for crafting my vision into a taut and exciting manuscript.

And thank you to any readers, new and old, who are following this series. I appreciate you all!

Chapter One

"You want me to do what?"

Ally studied Gordon in disbelief, sure she had misunderstood. Her boss avoided her gaze and took a sip of his wine.

About fifty employees were in attendance at the Shatter Sound private party. They piled together in groups, partaking of the open bar and available buffet. They swapped tales about past triumphs, the accounts getting taller with every beverage.

"Work with him and keep an eye on him at the same time. We got Dirk cheap for a reason, Ally. I'm not sold, but when a guy with his talent comes available, a smart businessman doesn't pass him up. Take him under your wing. Offer to help him get settled, show him the ropes. I don't have to tell you that we need Jess' album to hit. It would be smart for you to make sure that happened."

"Um…" She tried to appear casual by bracing herself on one of the poles bracketing the barstools by the dance floor. "Why'd we hire this guy if you don't trust him? Jess needs a boost, sure, but his reputation precedes him."

Gordon again didn't meet her eyes. "Reputations are good and bad. He can bring attention to us that we couldn't buy for any price. He exited Earthy Cry Records under questionable circumstances. Nothing was proven, but there were rumors about a huge screwup, maybe even missing money, and then Dirk was out of a job." He pinned her down with a glare. "We can use him, but we have to be careful. This is a good opportunity for you. The guy has talent. You can learn from him, get more skills to fatten up your résumé for that promotion you've been after."

"Is he...my boss?"

He squared his shoulders. The movement betrayed the stiffness along his spine. "Not exactly. It's more of a dotted-line thing. He's the vice president, and you're an executive director, but you report directly to me. Since you brought Jess into the fold, you get the credit. Look at this as a way to give her the best chance to succeed. Dirk Roberts has helped many fledgling artists hit big. He's got a knack for finding the right combination of product to keep the artist relevant. That's the reason I hired him. I'm counting on you to learn everything he can teach you and watch him at the same time. If he does anything suspicious, you are to tell me at once. Understood?"

She opened her mouth to say something she shouldn't but shut down her emotions before they could show. If he was asking her to take Dirk under her wing—if that was the key to getting her long-overdue promotion—then that was what she would do. If her years with the company weren't enough, she'd play this game until she got what she deserved.

"Just so I am clear. He's not my boss?" That would be something.

"Not as such, but you will be working together a lot."

Dotted line. Right. It seemed more like a long dash,

but at least he wasn't directly above her in the corporate structure. "I understand." *No, I don't.* "I'll work with him, of course. It ought to be interesting. With his reputation it's no wonder he was willing to take a job at a startup country label in Los Angeles." She studied her boss, who kept his attention focused away. "Do you think his being here will help generate press?"

He nodded, the grin on his face laced with avarice. "Why not? Reporters go where the story is. I'll make sure they pick up the trail of this one. Make it work. You always do."

"I'll get it done."

Dirk Roberts had not arrived. She knew everyone in the room. When she first learned he was coming, she should have checked him out online but hadn't been able to bring herself to. He was a roadblock, one more thing to get around in pursuit of her upward trajectory. Someday maybe she'd even own a company. A gal could dream.

Gordon set his plastic wine glass down and nodded to her. "Glad you're on board. He came cheap with all that experience, so discounted I couldn't say no. Got it?"

Now she was a spy, watching the man who had taken the job she'd earned. It would be on her shoulders if Dirk did anything wrong. "Sure, Gordon. I get it."

Ally refrained from saying what was on her mind. She glanced around the dark club, taking note of a new entrant who appeared to be someone who might go there regularly. He had on a cowboy hat and walked with that faint bow to his legs like a man who had just gotten off a horse. His face was covered in shadows, both from the club and the hat. He gazed around the club, his attention falling on Gordon. Nobody acknowledged him as he made his way toward them.

Ally tried to look away, but soon her attention focused on the man again. She had a sneaking suspicion about the identity of the mysterious stranger. He didn't have the look of a Los Angeles music industry professional—he belonged on a music video with his worn jeans and big-ass hat. Since the event was a private party, no strangers were invited. Therefore, this had to be Dirk Roberts. His appearance fit what little she had learned about him. Southerner. That was all she needed to know.

He swung around one of the divider poles and tapped Gordon on the shoulder. "Howdy, boss."

Howdy? Even before she took in the man speaking, Ally understood her quick assessment a few seconds before was correct. The man who had stolen the vice president of marketing gig that had been promised to her was here. Okay, maybe not promised to her, but implied. She'd earned it—and he'd taken it. All her hard work over the last five years proving herself to the higher-ups had come to nothing. Working late, going the extra mile, covering Gorgon's butt when needed, all of her efforts meant nothing. Dirk had what she coveted. To make it worse, he was a man with a tarnished reputation. Yet here they were.

Gordon pivoted, stepping back as he did so. "Dirk! Glad you could make it. Perfect timing. Ally Wilson, Dirk Roberts. Ally is part of the Shatter Sound marketing group. You'll be working together. We were just talking about you."

"Were you now? It wouldn't be the first time. Nice to meet you, ma'am." Dirk touched the fingertips of his right hand to his hat.

He was a giant of a man, almost as broad as he was tall. At least six feet five, he was sheer masculine power roped in a taut, muscular frame. He was a head taller than her, which was no small feat at her own five feet nine. His voice was gravel mixed with whiskey, tinged with a Southern drawl. It evoked images of bayou, low trees draped over the water, hot summer afternoons on the veranda with mint juleps.

His tanned face spoke of outdoor life, leaving lines bracketing his eyes and full mouth, a faint roughness to the skin. The close-cropped goatee added to the dangerous quality that lurked under the "aw shucks" persona.

Ally offered him her hand. He took it in his much larger one, shaking it in a perfunctory manner. His set jaw told her that he was expecting a cool reaction.

"What's Ally short for?" he asked.

He filled her vision with his large frame. Her heart stuttered in an unexpected reaction. She tried to ignore the tingles of awareness the scrape of his callused palm left on her flesh. "My name? Short for Alanna. It's Gaelic for noble or fair, or something like that."

Clearing her throat, she was relieved to find that her nerves were outwardly steady. He was standing close to them in order to be heard in the bar. Heat drifted off him like a warm embrace. Ally almost swayed toward him before she caught herself. A spicy scent that might have been his cologne tickled her nostrils. She wouldn't have thought cowboys indulged in fragrance. She kept her face neutral, despite the pinging of her nerve endings. "Nice to meet you too. I'm glad you've joined our team. We need all the help we can get." *Liar. The job should have been yours.*

A muscle worked in the back of his jaw as his gaze darted around the room. If she was reading his body language correctly, he'd rather be anywhere but here.

Maybe he'd go back home and leave the VP slot open for her to grab.

"Mind if I call you Alanna? It suits you better." He tilted his beer toward her.

"Whatever makes you happy." She tried not to shiver when he met her gaze. That was not going to happen. Not with this guy.

Green eyes with dark, almost-black rims peered out from behind the hat. It shaded his face, rendering his expression unreadable. She had to imagine that was on purpose. Nice trick. She would adopt it, except she looked crappy in hats. He was wearing a black shirt, blue Wranglers, a belt with a large silver buckle, and black cowboy boots on his feet. As she thought before, Dirk Roberts would not have been out of place on stage anywhere in Nashville. Not here.

"Great. Now that I've introduced you, I'll leave you to get to know each other," Gordon said. He patted Ally on the shoulder and moved to the bar where Robin, the head of sales, stood.

Time to do her job. "Welcome to Los Angeles— and our record label. How long have you been here?"

"Three days," he answered.

"How do you like it so far? Big change from Nashville, I imagine."

Hooking his free thumb into his belt, he took a drink of his beer. "It's different," he said with no inflection. "Big. Crowded."

When he moved, a sandy blond ponytail swung

away from his back, then settled against his shirt. She wouldn't have expected it in a man whose entire appearance screamed of someone who would be more at home in open spaces. He had no business being anywhere near Los Angeles. The low rumble of his tone left her little doubt of his disdain for her adopted city.

"I've never been to the South, but I can understand what you're saying. I'm from Connecticut myself. When I first got here, this city was bigger than I could imagine. Sometimes I felt like I could drive forever and never hit the limits. You get used to the distances, if it's any comfort. Plus, the urban sprawl peters out once we hit the mountains."

One side of his mouth tilted up, revealing even white teeth. His smile transformed him, taking years off his face. She'd guessed he was near forty, but his grin took that down five years. Then it faded, the taciturn expression reasserting itself. Ally tried not to let the frisson of awareness show. If this were anyone else, she'd make her exit. Unexpected attraction or not.

"I have no intention of getting used to it," he said with a husky tone. "I'm a country boy through and through. This city is where I work, that's all."

His words had a bitter undertone, as if he had tasted something sour. She could almost hear his assessment of the bar they were in. *A cheap imitation of the real thing. Fucking Los Angeles.*

She went silent, gazing out across the bar. As she watched, someone in one of the groups pointed to Dirk. Even from the distance, she could read their faces. Dirk's reputation had preceded him.

Since leaving wasn't an option, she steeled herself. "Come on." She gestured toward the bar. "Let me introduce you to your new co-workers."

His hand shot out and grasped her wrist, stilling her progress. "That can keep. They don't want to meet me." The jerk of his chin encompassed the entire bar. His face once again settled into taciturn lines before he let her go. "I wouldn't have come to this shindig, but Gordon insisted. The only thing that changes people's minds is time. No need to force the issue." His features shifted, the hardening of his jaw pulling the goatee down.

"Okay." The skin under his fingers tingled. The lingering heat of his hand made goose bumps erupt on her forearm. Ally rubbed at the spot. "Then let's talk business. I'll get you up to speed. Our focus is new country artist Jessica Baker. I've been working on her campaign. Jess is in the studio right now. I hope you have some time to come listen to the album and make a recommendation."

"Sure. I don't need to do that to work on a campaign, but if it will help, I can turn up." His drawl thickened, and he eased back until his face was hooded by his hat again. Crossing his arms, he rocked away from her. "Y'all understand what you're in for hiring me."

She turned her face away in case her wayward thoughts showed. "I wasn't given a choice." The words were as close as she dared come to revealing her bitterness at his hire. "Gordon didn't ask for my opinion. I will show you what needs to be done. It's my job."

He nodded. The short, curt movement was accompanied by a jerky motion as he took his tablet out of a satchel she hadn't noticed before. "Fair enough.

Let's get to it. Tell me about Jess. Stuff I can't find online."

A few intrepid folks were on the dance floor, attempting line dances. Most were at the bar, taking advantage of the free beer and wine while they still could. If she wasn't afraid that she'd look stupid, Ally wouldn't have minded trying the line dances. She bet this hulking giant knew them all.

"Jess. I'll start with the basics. She's twenty-five and a mezzo-soprano who writes most of her own songs. A lot of artists have the reputation of being unpretentious, but she actually is. Performing hasn't made her egotistical—yet. She's been writing since she was fifteen years old and playing clubs since she was eighteen."

"Sounds like you like her." Dirk gazed at her with those dazzling green eyes.

Her breath caught again. He made quick notations as she spoke. Memory keys, if she had to guess.

"I do. It's made handling her marketing simple so far."

"Glad you've gotten a head start on that. Let me see what I can do, now that I'm here. She's at a disadvantage being here instead of Nashville, but that's nothing video calls can't solve. She good on her feet?"

"Very. She's got an answer for everything."

"Great. That will help. I checked her out online. She can come across tough in her pictures. If that's not right, we have to change that. What are your thoughts?" His hand poised over the tablet showed he was waiting for her answer.

His eyes glittered like emeralds. Ally shoved the awareness away. "Good insight. I have to agree. I think she should go for the girl-next-door, but she also likes being a bit of a hardcase." She snorted and covered her mouth to suppress her discomfort. "Sorry. That's the best I can do. I'm sure you can reel off dozens of classic artists she resembles, but this is new to me."

White teeth flashed below the rim of his Stetson. "I got it," he assured her. His goatee twitched.

The blond ponytail swung forward again as he moved. His hands were dusted with blond hair shining over the tan skin. Trimmed nails rested on top of the long fingers.

A man like this would never ever get a manicure. In a town where appearances often meant everything, this rugged giant might have been appealing if he weren't such a sourpuss.

"We doing a video?"

"Not right now," she said. "The budget is minuscule for this first release. A video, one that would get played, would put a strain on our finances. There's no point."

His mouth moved in silent contemplation as he wrote something else on his pad. "I've seen her on social media. She's damned cute—we should play that up. Lose the rough spots and gussy her up. We'll do something, even if we post it for free. I'll work on that. What about a fan club? She got her name up on all the sites?"

She nodded. "She's had the domain name for years. There's a website already in place. We are working on hiring a webmaster to add bells and whistles. All that is covered. She's got a loyal fan base that we're building on. Her manager has all the details, but I stay involved."

"Good." He replaced the tablet in the satchel. "Thanks for the update. We've got a lot of work ahead of us, but it's good you're on the team."

Ally tilted her head, trying to decipher what his words meant. Then she gave up the attempt. She'd have to ask him to be sure, and she didn't do that sort of thing. Asking implied caring, which inferred needing others. That wasn't for her, no way, no how. She had one person she relied on.

On the team. His team. Not hers. "I'm excited for the next steps." What Gordon asked her to do stuck in her craw, but she pushed through the resentment. "Do you have any friends in Los Angeles?"

"Hell no. Not anymore. I'm on speaking terms with you, Gordon, and the guard at that box called an 'efficiency apartment' they got me shoehorned into."

"You're at those month-to-month rentals in Studio City?" The apartments were dark, functional, gigantic complexes designed for temporary visitors, not a man as big as Dirk.

"Yeah."

"I'm amazed you fit."

"I don't," he said, his voice clipped.

"I bet." She went silent again, watching him as he half turned from her, staring toward the pool table.

He wasn't charming, despite the surface Southern politeness. He held himself on a razor's edge, the hat hiding his face. Something about that movement made her wonder what he was thinking.

Gordon came up behind her and clapped her on the back. "How are you two getting along?"

Dirk turned toward Gordon, but his visage was impossible to read under the hat. The move had to be done on purpose. The man could be hiding any expression under those shadows. "Miss Wilson here was catching me up to speed. Or is it Mrs.?"

Whether his gaze went to her bare left hand or not, Ally couldn't tell. "Miss or just Ally. Alanna. There's no Mr. Wilson or boyfriend or anything."

You're a Moped, Ally. Good enough to ride, but not something you'd be seen with. The voice with its slight British accent stung, even from two years distant. She shook her head to loosen the memory.

"That's why she's such a great employee. She can always work late when needed." Gordon's shrill voice was too loud.

She wondered how many drinks he'd had. Thank goodness HR had arranged for rideshares. "Gordon..."

"Except Sundays, unless it's an emergency. Football, isn't that right, Ally? You love that crazy game. I have no idea why."

"Connecticut doesn't have a pro football team. I grew up with the Patriots. What's not to love? They had an amazing run."

Gordon fixed his attention on Dirk and then back to her. "Do you still have those parties every Sunday? Paige comes over to hang out, right? She's the assistant I'm going to assign to Dirk. It would be a good time to...you know."

Oh no. No, no. He couldn't be suggesting—but the raised eyebrows and expectant gaze left her no doubt what Gordon meant.

She was going to lose this one. She had a job to do. Getting Dirk on her territory might help. She mourned the loss of her relaxed Sunday but then squared her shoulders. She'd done worse things for the company. At least he'd be pleasant to look at.

"Good idea, Gordon. Paige will be there, and it would make sense to introduce her to her new boss before Monday since she couldn't come tonight." She pasted on her best, brightest grin and faced her newest assignment. "Dirk, did you ever play football?"

He nodded, a grin splitting his face and lifting the goatee. "Sure, you kiddin'? Guy my size? In Georgia? All the Roberts boys were tagged for the team. I played in high school and college, chose not to try for the pros. Right tackle mostly, outside linebacker in a pinch. Why?"

"Because on Sunday a group of us are going to get together at my house. We'll watch the games, barbecue, and have fun." She took a deep breath. "You're new in town. Don't spend your weekend alone cooped up. Join us. You just can't root against the Pats."

He was silent for so long she continued in a rush, the words tumbling out of her mouth.

"If you need somewhere to go, come over. We're going to be spending a lot of time together, so what Gordon suggested makes sense. My friends are great; you'll like them." She wondered if he could detect the lie.

She watched him as he tensed again, emotion boiling over his face. A world of hurt flowed through his face and then was gone.

"You're a football fan?" he said, the tension easing from his shoulders.

"Yep. Patriots. Since I'm from Connecticut."

"You could have gone with New York. Jets or Giants are good—although not lately. I'm an Atlanta Falcons man myself. That's very kind of you. I'll take you up on it if you don't mind. Much obliged."

Gordon grinned and let out a breath. "See you Monday." He retreated again, leaving her to face the chaos of her Sunday.

She turned back to Dirk. "I'm happy to do it. No need to bring anything unless you've got a beverage you prefer. Otherwise, there will be enough food for one of the teams. Just one more thing, though. The boys tend to get loud. Paige and I join in. Fair warning."

Dirk's grin flickered back into life. "Watch a Georgia game sometime if you think you're loud. I'm pleased as punch to get the invite. See you then."

Ally was pretty sure she wasn't "pleased as punch," but she said nothing.

Chapter Two

Dirk threw his pickup into park in front of a house with a New England Patriots flag mounted on a flagpole that jutted out from the porch.

He'd been to Los Angeles before—of course he had. When called to the West Coast on business trips, he'd done what he had to do and then gotten out as fast as possible. The dry air assaulted his senses. He'd never gone beyond what was necessary to get in and back out. Of all the cities he figured he'd wind up in, Los Angeles was the last place he expected to be. He'd spent his entire life in the South, never desiring to spend too much time in a city north of Virginia or west of Texas. Yet here he was. For now.

The neighborhood could have been ripped from one of Nashville's suburbs, plus the palms and minus the oaks. All the houses were the same, starter homes that had the appearance of being built sometime in the middle of the last century. Those that hadn't been remodeled, anyway. A pecan tree laden with birds was visible a couple of addresses down. The faint hum of the main street two blocks away reminded him how close he was to traffic, but no cars moved on this one besides his. Instead of sidewalks, sloping pavement met the street. A quiet hush descended around him as he absorbed the calm of her neighborhood.

Her house had a patch of grass that would need to

be replaced in the spring, two walnut trees, and a large crepe myrtle tree in the middle of the yard. A long driveway wound along the right side of the house, ending in a two-car garage. The house was a light blue color—a blue that complemented her eyes. The woman was a mystery. When they met less than two days ago, any fool could have recognized she was on edge. The tightened shoulders and straight back had told him that whatever she was thinking, they weren't good thoughts. The lush curves of her body had been accentuated by a loose-fitting olive-green shirt and black pants that skimmed her figure. One that called to every masculine inch of him.

He shook himself out of that unwelcome awareness. He wasn't staying in this hellhole any longer than he had to. He wasn't about to fuck it up by bending the first sexy woman he found over his desk. This invite was a setup if there ever was one. He had no doubt Alanna had been told to keep an eye on him. Hell, if it had been him, he would have done the same. If Marlon hadn't suggested it, then he would have. Those days, and that friendship, were long over. He had no business being here. He had a reputation to restore and didn't want to deal with a stuck-up Yankee spy.

Why in tarnation are you here, then? His plan for Sunday had been going down to the sports bar in Media City Center and take in the games, not placing himself in the line of fire. The woman was not in his plans. A vision of her lush curves danced through his brain. The tightening of his jeans gave him an answer. Hell. He needed a woman but not this one.

He slammed the door and started up her driveway. In front of the door was a welcome mat that told visitors "wipe your hooves" with a pig waggling its finger. Dirk took a breath and then rapped on the door.

Her face was as pretty as ever even in the daytime with the sun shining on her skin. Her hair was honey and sunshine, the ends swinging from a blunt cut. Eyes the color of the ocean met his with no sign of what she was feeling. Her lips were so red they had to be tattooed, but they sure would be good wrapped around him. He shook his head. Stupid thing to think about. *Get your mind out of the gutter, Roberts.*

He should make an excuse and go.

"Come on in," she said. "Welcome."

He held out the paper grocery bag to her, cursing the fact that he'd worn close-fitting jeans. Her clothing, as it had been on Friday, was simple. The loose-fitting garments concealed her curves rather than enhancing them. A polo shirt with a Patriots logo above the left breast draped across her body, the inviting tops of her breasts in the button-down placket catching his attention. Her feet were bare, long toes with unvarnished nails peeking out from under curved calves. A sudden memory of Bobbie Jo, his first girlfriend, sitting together with him on his parents' front porch, her bare feet swinging as they rocked, dashed through him.

Alanna's house wasn't a big place, maybe fourteen hundred square feet total. The foyer he stood in led to a hallway with a kitchen visible beyond it, a dining room on his right, and the living room to his left. The main area held an L-shaped couch in russet tones, a ceiling fan in the middle, and plush area rugs. The entertainment unit was on the far wall, with a thirty-five-inch TV and electronic components. A faint scent of vanilla tinged the air.

Three strangers sat in the living room, two men and a woman. He appraised the men, taking their measure as he was sure they took his. One of the two stood out, a man named Craig in his early thirties who was tall and model handsome, with a smooth exterior. This was one to watch. He might have a claim on the woman Dirk didn't wish to be attracted to.

The other woman turned out to be Paige, his new assistant. She looked about five years younger than him, with auburn brown hair and small features. She greeted him with a casual wave, her attention focused on the game.

He had yet to take the measure of the other man. He didn't show much curiosity when Dirk walked in. California men were strange, so that didn't mean anything. Dirk ignored the part of him that wanted to rearrange Craig's face if he was her man. That was foolhardy, at best.

"Nice place. Looks cozy."

He hadn't noticed it in the bar, but a set of four, small, faded scars lining the top and side of her right eye caught his attention. He frowned, unsure of what kind of situation would cause that sort of damage. He had no right to ask. Pain flickered over her face, like a wound that had healed but still burned in the night.

Curiosity could kill more than cats, and he kept his tongue. He had no intention of getting close to anyone in this town. He would do his time, fix the mess he'd left behind, and he was gone. He had no business even being here, let alone speculate on what was going on behind Alanna's shuttered gaze.

A hearty arrangement of snacks was on the table.

Scrambled eggs, hash browns, sausages, and bacon lay in plain white dishware on top of a Patriots tablecloth. He grunted, just suppressing the warmth he felt at this generous array.

"Guess I didn't need to bring anything," he said, gesturing to the table.

Craig glanced over. "I never do. There's no point. She makes enough for an army." His smile was indulgent, without heat. That was the way he liked it.

"I said you didn't, but I appreciate it anyway."

NFL paraphernalia decorated the living room. Crepe-paper NFL-logo streamers fanned out from the combination light/fan on the ceiling, twisted and pinned in the four corners of the room. Yellow cut-up squares of cloth suggesting referee penalty flags were heaped in the middle of the coffee table. A weighted flag was sprawled on the ground. A miniature 18-wheeler Patriots logo truck was on the shelf on top of the TV. A Tom Brady bobblehead was next to it, as well as a Patriots bear and a logo nerf football. Patriots clings decorated the paned window in front of the couch. A large one dominated the center, and several smaller ones were along the sides. Light caught the clings and reflected the colors into the room, casting red, white, and blue shadows across the fireplace wall.

Dirk cocked an eyebrow at Ally. "You meant it when you said you were a fan." His tone was neutral, giving no clue to his meaning. "I like it."

A sudden whoop distracted them, and they turned to the TV. Craig was pumping his fists in the air. "Interception, baby," he cried. "Run it back, all the way."

After the play was over, Craig turned his attention

to Ally. "Say, where's your Cap jersey today, Als?"

Dirk's attention shifted from the too-handsome man back to Alanna.

"Cap as in Gino Cappelletti. Boston Patriot from 1960 to 1970 and my dad's favorite player. Dad loved football back then and still does. He's from Boston. The Pats are his team. I get my fandom from him."

"Mom wasn't a fan?"

She shook her head. "Hell no. She should have been a flower child, but she was born a little too late. Football was way too brutal for her." She turned her attention to her friend. "Sorry to disappoint, Craig. I didn't have a chance to do laundry this week. You wouldn't like smelling it right now."

"My dad liked Bob Berry, Falcons quarterback from 1968 to 1972. Got a jersey, but it's in storage. Next year."

When she suggested they watch the game outside on her outdoor television on her back lanai, he considered making his exit. He'd done his time. Instead, Dirk joined Ally and Craig in the backyard, stepping out to a covered lanai. An herb garden swayed on the left, and an empty hammock beckoned behind the grill. A light breeze made the leaves on the back poplar trees sway. Sparrows tweeted from the telephone wires.

"What's the weather like in Nashville?" she asked Dirk.

"Thirties to forties," he replied. "Freezes sometimes. Rains a lot this time of year." He gestured to the sky with his index finger. "It ain't like this." He opened his arms wide. "This isn't natural."

"Hey, Dirk, catch this."

One of Alanna's nerf footballs sailed toward Dirk. He grabbed it with one hand before tossing it back in Craig's direction. Craig's sneakered feet sank into the soft earth as he caught the ball.

"It's still damp," she said. "All that rain we got last week is still seeping into the water table. You needed a rowboat to get across my backyard."

"I assumed you didn't get weather here."

"Hah. I assumed that too until I moved out here. You know what they say about it never raining in Southern California."

Dirk took a moment to recognize the reference. The band was—the name escaped him.

"Anyway, we have crazy weather sometimes. Comes down in buckets, then it's eighty degrees."

A palm tree waved in the breeze. The fronds that moved with it caught his attention. "Bet those things are a problem." He pointed toward the ground where one of the fronds lay in the grass, its shaft dotted with thick thorns.

Ally glanced at it. "Oh yeah. They've got these thorns on the sides that will rip your hands apart." She gestured to the wires going from her house to the telephone pole in the back corner of her yard. "In the Santa Anas last year, I woke up in the wee hours after something crashed to the ground. When I went outside, those wires must have had ten fronds hanging on them. I had to get them down, which wasn't whole lot of fun dealing with them balanced on a ladder in the middle of the night. I had to get the things down before they could mess up the electricity to my garage."

"Santa Anas?"

"You haven't read about the Santa Ana winds?"

she asked.

He shook his head.

She grinned and continued. "They scared me the first time I experienced them. There aren't winds like that in Glastonbury. That first winter we had them, the winds were so hot and dry I couldn't put enough moisturizer on my body or lip balm on my mouth. A couple of times I was worried my car was going to blow off the freeway from the force of the winds. It's a dangerous time for fires. Paige always says that whenever the Santa Anas came around, it's earthquake weather. So far she's been wrong."

He grunted when she finished. "I hope she continues to be wrong." He tried not to notice the way the sun played over her hair and face, making her shine in its rays.

"Me too." She waved a hand toward her friend. "Someday she'll be right, but not today. I like it here. Right, Paige?"

Paige looked up at the sound of her name, and her forehead furrowed.

"Earthquakes. Dry weather."

A smile crossed Paige's face. "Dry as the desert and just as hot. Earthquake weather."

"Shush with that. Lalalalalala, I don't hear you." Alanna put her hands over her ears and made a delightful motion with her tongue that made his body tighten.

"You started it," Paige grumbled before turning back to the game.

"My mama would say hush your mouth. She used that for most everything." He cleared his throat. His mother wouldn't know what to make of this woman.

He wasn't sure he did.

****

Ally wouldn't admit to anyone except herself that she had been watching Dirk since the minute he arrived at her door. In daylight his eyes were a searing, penetrating green that spoke of the thickness of forest leaves. The sun landed on his face, turning his tanned skin molten brown. A hint of silver shot through the goatee. His hair was pulled back in a ponytail and covered by a baseball cap with a car manufacturer logo on it. What would that hair be like draped over his shoulders...or hers? A blue, sleeveless denim shirt and Wranglers completed the outfit. The clothing followed the lines of his muscular body, drawing her eye to the broad expanse of his chest.

No visitor to her house had ever been taller than the separator between her foyer and the living room until today. Nobody who had to duck as he exited through her back door and into her yard. She was glad she'd suggested the move to the outdoors. At least her lanai was tall enough to accommodate him.

"Have you had enough? Do you want me to open the wine you brought?" He'd been in her place for an hour, and she was running out of things to say. Paige and Vinnie continued to watch the game from the patio table after they all migrated outside.

"Naw, it's too early for drinking. That wine is for you. I'll take some coffee, though."

She retreated to the kitchen, almost grateful to be removed from the man. This was not how she wanted her Sunday to go. The thought that her usurper would also be the most appealing man she'd met in years was disagreeable. She'd been prepared to dislike the new

23

VP, not want to kiss him.

Her #20 Gino Cappelletti Boston Patriots replica throwback jersey was her usual attire on game days. It made her body a shapeless tank, which was fine when it was just her pals. Today, she'd succumbed to vanity and opted for the knit top instead.

Returning with the coffee, Ally handed it to Dirk and backed away.

She tried to ignore the knot in her stomach. What this gruff man thought of her and her friends shouldn't make any difference. Dirk had taken the job meant for her, and now her future was coupled to his. At least he had commented favorably on her party.

This game is so uncivilized. I don't understand what you see in it. This food is—what are you serving again?

The echo of a past disastrous party rang through her. She remembered a tousled blond-haired man studying the television with a sneer while using his cell phone to dial the local sushi place for different edibles.

She shook her head. That had been years ago. No point in dwelling on it.

The referees calling out penalties and the sportscasters analyzing the plays distracted her. She turned to watch the talking heads break down a blocked punt.

"My wife hated football." Dirk followed her gaze to the screen. "She was part of the reason I didn't try for pro. It scared her."

Before she could respond, a runner broke free and ran down the field. Paige and Vinnie shouted at the screen as the runner bolted into the end zone.

"No way." Vinnie was on his feet. "That was so

pass interference." A yellow flag landed on the brick in front of the TV.

"Naw. The receiver had no chance of catching the ball." Dirk made the statement with authority, and Vinnie shot him a curious glance but said nothing further. Paige's attention went from Dirk to Ally before she turned her focus back to the television.

She'd read about a wife and also was aware he was divorced. When she researched him after she met him the first time, his marital status hadn't mattered. She shot the too-compelling man a quick grin. "I've got to agree with Dirk. That was a legal hit."

A spirited discussion of the pros and cons of football referees started. Dirk's rumble carried an air of authority to it, his bass cutting through the air. Ally could listen to him all day.

She swallowed, focusing on the TV screen but seeing him in her peripheral vision. All she had to do was sway forward to lean in and smell him. His powerful body was so near that it wouldn't take much for her to reach over, put her hands across his thighs, touch him...

Nope. No sirree, Bob. She'd been attracted to inappropriate men before, but this had to take a prize for most self-destructive. Even if he by some astonishing miracle was also attracted to her, that way led to nothing but monsters. *Here be tygers.* If she wanted to blow her life up, then she would keep at it.

Dirk would never be attracted to her. That wasn't who Ally Wilson was. Good enough to sleep with and pal around with but not built for forever. She twitched, past hurts searing inside her.

The game resumed, and Dirk stepped away from

the lanai. "I've been meaning to ask y'all. What's with the pigs?" He pointed with an index finger bent at the top knuckle to a spinning pig windmill in the middle of the yard.

Heat crawled up her cheeks. *I can't believe you display those pigs, Ally. It's undignified.*

"Ally is obsessed with them," Craig said. He tossed the ball in the air as he spoke.

She stuck her tongue out at her friend, crinkling her nose. "Don't mince words, Craig—tell Dirk what you really think." She directed her attention to Dirk. "When I was a kid, I loved the book Charlotte's Web. Wilbur the pig was so great. One day I found a pig figurine at a store and had to have it. It went from there." She crossed her arms, aware of her defensive posture but unable to correct it. "Not piggy banks or cookie jars, actual pigs. The pinker the better. I wouldn't say obsessed is the right word, just a deep like."

Dirk grinned, that crooked gesture mesmerizing her. "Belinda collected magnets herself. Our fridge was covered with them. We had to start putting them on the side of the stove because we ran out of room."

She let out a breath. Belinda must be the ex-wife. He sounded amused, even indulgent.

It didn't matter.

"Dirk, think fast," Craig said.

He chucked the football across the yard, and Dirk reached up to catch it with an automatic gesture.

"Don't y'all have a real football? This bitty thing is too easy to catch." He tossed the thing to Ally, who caught it and then dropped it to the patio table under the lanai.

She was silent for a minute. "Sure. Hang on." She

retreated to the den and came out a second later with a regulation-size pigskin. "Here." She threw it underhand to him.

He flung the football to Craig. Craig hurled it back in a quick release. Dirk caught it as he might have in college, arms out, the ball landing as he was hauling it into his body.

"We usually play with the Nerf ball because Ally can't catch."

Dirk stared at the regulation football before tossing it under the lanai where it quivered before coming to rest. She watched it land before turning to him.

"You said your dad loved football." He gestured to the table with his chin. "Didn't he teach you how to play?"

"He did," she replied. "He does. However, my parents divorced when I was eight. Mom got primary custody."

"What about school? Y'all didn't have anything coed?"

She let her hair fall forward to cover her eyes. Her mouth twisted, and she was unable to speak for what seemed like an eternity.

Scum, scum, smelly dirty scum.

"No. Marta and I didn't run with the popular crowd."

She didn't raise her head until she was sure the bleakness she couldn't hide was gone.

A handful of her friends knew her backstory, and she'd learned the hard way that few understood. Of those, fewer cared. She had to be careful who she trusted.

That did not include Dirk. No matter how

mouthwatering his butt was in jeans.

"You a Red Sox fan too?" he asked, his eyebrows lifting.

"Sure. The day they won the World Series was one of the best days of my life. Game four I met Daddy in Kenmore Square near Fenway Park. We watched them sweep and then danced in the streets. Dad was ecstatic."

"Damn Yankee."

"Damn Yankees," she retorted. "Redneck."

"I'm not a redneck," he replied, his lips tilting up. "I'm a good ole boy."

She wasn't going to ask what that meant.

It shouldn't matter.

Chapter Three

Ally paused before knocking on Dirk's open door. She wasn't sure of the wisdom of what she was about to do, but he'd been brought on to problem solve. Besides, she'd told him she wanted him to hear Jess' album. Now was the perfect time.

He turned his head to gaze at the new arrival before motioning for her to come in.

Marketing plans, a new-release book, plus medical and dental information littered his desk. Behind him, on a credenza, was his digital player as well as a CD player and a smattering of CDs. She expected traditional, modern country, and Southern rock. She didn't anticipate Led Zeppelin, Guns N' Roses, Van Halen, and Foo Fighters. CDs were an anachronism, and she liked him better for that throwback touch.

Dirk uncoiled his body from its crouched position in front of a large white bulletin board propped up against the wall. He had a timeline for Jess' Shatter Sound release, when the artwork, the liner notes, and the photo shoot needed to be completed notated as action items. A list of the catalog artists Dirk was targeting for re-releases was scrawled in a ragged line down the board. She had a similar one in her smaller office.

He had on a black shirt and jeans with a Stetson resting on the desk. If it had been anyone else, she would have laughed. She would not do so in front of this stoic giant.

"What can I help you with, Alanna?" He folded his arms across his chest and observed her from his greater height.

If he intended it to be intimidating, he'd succeeded. He was so damned big. She tried to control her frisson of anxiety, but her gaze darted around, searching for a safe place to land. She wanted to mutter at him to *stop it* but wouldn't give him the satisfaction. Hopeful vice presidents didn't show fear. Neither did executive directors. She was better than that.

He said nothing, just watched her. She studied his whiteboard before sliding her gaze to his and then away. "I'm here about Jess. You got a couple of minutes?"

At his brisk nod, she continued.

"I hoped you would have an hour or so to come down to the studio. I've been helping her manager. One of Jessica's songs isn't working." She nodded to the piles of paper, wishing she hadn't come. "If you're too busy…"

"What's going on?"

"The song has all the right components, but it just doesn't work. Maybe you could listen to it and give feedback. The rumor is you used to be great at that. Fixing songs, that is."

His nostrils flared like he was going to grunt out a reply. "I'm dying to get into the sunshine and away from that desk for a spell, so you got yourself a deal." He moved toward her.

Ally backed up, and he stopped where he was.

"Be a good opportunity to hear the thing anyway."

"Cool," she exclaimed. Part of her longed to feel his body heat, but he could not know that. "I can drive."

"Remind me what you drive."

Her eyebrows furrowed at the question. "Four-door sedan, why?"

"Sure I'm gonna fit?"

She wanted to laugh. She could not do so. "There's a sunroof. We'll just stick the rest of you out that way."

He grunted in a sound that might have been a laugh.

When they got to her car, he removed his hat to clear the roof and then pushed the passenger seat all the way back before scrunching down to fit. She couldn't do much to ease his discomfort. The old Ally, the people-pleaser, would have been surfing the car sites to buy something bigger. The new Ally would refrain from such nonsense. She would do what she had to do to get the title she deserved, but that was all.

She would even share the title with him. She wasn't greedy. The company could support two vice presidents. They could call her something different.

She ignored the part of her that sought to break through his reserve. She was no longer the queen of lost causes or of trying to fit herself into an expected mold to get a man to love her. Dirk would have to be a project for someone else. Not her. She was only interested in him professionally.

She loaded the music player into its dock, and the first song came up.

Lifting an eyebrow at her, he said, "You like hip hop? I pictured you as a rock and roll gal."

"I'd argue that all music is good, but yeah, I do. It pays to keep current. You never know who you might work on next."

"There's a reason I lived in Nashville. It's not my style."

When he reverted to that stone-statue appearance, saying nothing, she suppressed a giggle. That would have been beyond inappropriate. "Rap and hip hop have an important place in our culture." She allowed herself a grin at his continued stoic face. "Not even Grandmaster Flash or the early pioneers?"

He turned his head to the side, a motion that she'd learned in the last week meant he was finding his words. Maybe she had learned a thing or two about his body language.

"You got me there. I respect him for being an innovator in the field. He led where others followed. It's like Hank Senior and Buck Owens. Without them the rest would never have happened. 'The Message' and 'White Lines,' though amazing, are depressing."

She focused on her dashboard to hide her surprise at his awareness of the '70s innovator. She sang part of the chorus, shooting him a quick glance at the same time.

He did laugh then, finishing the line. The single word rumbled through the car.

Gesturing to the player on the console between them, she glanced at him. "Pick something, then."

Her collection was a mix of rock, hard rock, hair bands, country, and rap. He kept thumbing through them without making a selection.

"What are you searching for? Waylon, Willie—something old school? Sorry, Dirk, I've got the basics but no Loretta Lynn or Johnny Cash or anything."

He shook his head, and his goatee drew down. He

might have had hurt on his face if he were someone else. Dirk was a stoic giant of a man. The slings and arrows of one woman should bounce right off him.

"That's not what I was after. I was trying to find *Nevermind* by Nirvana. Or something by Pearl Jam, Alice in Chains, Soundgarden, or any of the popular grunge bands from the '90s. None of that is here. There a reason?"

She gestured to the device. "I only have a couple for research and even then, not many. I'm biased. I heard what happened when Nirvana broke. Their ascension stalled the careers of most of the older musicians I met. No grunge for me. Glad that depressing phase is over. Give me big hair and spandex over flannel and staring at your shoes any day of the week."

His chuckle at the old joke sent curls of warmth through her body.

"I've been trying to catch up on country, and I'm finding that it crosses over into rock quite a bit. That works for me. I don't like bluegrass. I know that much."

"Me either. It's Daddy's favorite, though. Mama has to leave the room when he puts it on."

Universal Studios was on their right when they crossed the bridge over the 170 Freeway. Ally turned left onto Cahuenga Blvd., which quickly became Highland Avenue.

The Hollywood Hills were lush and green, heavy with vegetation. Later in the blazing heat of summer, those same hills would dry out and turn brown, creating a risk of fire. For now, they reminded her a little of home.

Dirk's thumb stilled on the music player, his mouth quirking up in a grin. "Man, I haven't heard this one in years."

The strains of Def Leppard's "Rock of Ages" began. She sang the opening lines under her breath, delighted by the choice. She glanced at him but said nothing.

The Hollywood Bowl was on the right as they came down the hill. Its gates were shut for winter, but the sign still stood out on the hillside. When she merged into dense Hollywood traffic on Highland Avenue, she noted that his body stiffened.

"Enough cars for you?" she asked.

His hand slid along the armrest and took the handle. "Nashville has rush hour downtown, but the sheer volume here is unbelievable."

She wove her sedan between lanes with the ease of long familiarity but slowed when his grip on the handle tightened.

Slow down. Are you crazy? Women drivers are all the same. We should have taken my car. It's a luxury car, not this American horror.

The voice of Connor faded as she got into a lane and stayed there. Dirk eased his grip and sat back in his seat. They passed Hollywood and Highland where a massive outdoor mall stood in imposing concrete. As they passed it, she pointed to her right where tourists and locals dressed in costume milled on the sidewalk.

"Mann's Chinese Theater, formerly Grauman's and the site of all the hand and footprints, is on our right, halfway down the block. You should go into Hollywood sometime and do the tourist thing. It's way cleaner than it used to be. Everyone should see the landmark, even transplants."

She was talking too much, trying to drown out her awareness of his heated body, trying to distract herself from what was running through her mind. Thoughts of tangling her hands in that ponytail to determine its softness. Of running her fingers over his goatee to see if it was soft or prickly. Darker fantasies focused below the waist. She had to be crazy to think anything along those lines. She wasn't even sure she liked the guy.

"Maybe." His voice was cool and just this side of polite.

The remainder of the drive to the studio was conducted in silence, accompanied by the hard driving beat of the Def Leppard songs. Dirk tapped his fingers on the armrest in a manner that indicated he was familiar with the album.

He stretched when they got out of the car, his joints popping. She tried not to look at him as they made their way to the studio.

He opened the door for her, then ducked to clear the top of the jamb, placing his hat back on his head when he was through.

"Do you ever feel like Gulliver among the Lilliputians?" she asked, watching his large frame fill the doorway as he stepped through. "I always felt big until I met you."

"Every day," he replied with that same cool tone he'd had earlier. "Sometimes more like Frankenstein, without the bolts. You're a tiny bit of a thing to me." He gestured for her to go ahead of him.

She wondered at his compliment, if that's what she could construe it as, but left her questions where they belonged. Nowhere.

The studio had a mixing board to the right as they walked in, but nobody was currently at the levers. The musicians and technicians were in the break room, talking or some playing video games on their phones. Ally gave them a wave as she entered and was greeted by a chorus of welcomes in return.

Jessica was in the middle of the studio, running through some vocal tracks with the producer. Instruments were scattered around the studio. At their approach Jess stopped and took off the headphones. She motioned the two of them into the room. Ally took a deep breath as they got closer to the singer.

"Jess, this is Dirk Roberts."

Jessica's startled glance reminded Ally of all the rumors.

"I've heard about you," she said, a myriad of emotions tearing across her face.

****

The blow that came out of nowhere was always the one that took people down. Dirk had expected it, and a part of him welcomed it. Jessica's apprehension was the perfect reminder of what he faced. Even recognizing that Alanna was a spy, and the situation a setup, didn't stop him from enjoying his time with her. He lapped it up like a damned dog is what he did.

This was better.

"I'm not surprised," he said, his voice gruff. "Unless that matters, how about we figure out what's wrong with your song?" He waited to see if Jess would refuse.

After she and Alanna exchanged a glance, the woman gave a minute shake of her head. Dirk should have been grateful.

Yeah—he was grateful. So much so.

He had them play it three times, conscious of Ally watching on. Then he waved for the musicians in the break room to come back in. Once they had, he removed the electric guitar from its stand and then adjusted the strap until the guitar was comfortable across his body. He had played enough instruments in his time to be confident it would work.

"I got a notion to try something," he said, checking the tuning of the guitar as he spoke. "This song, 'Susan the Magician,' it's about a woman who doesn't think she can measure up to a prettier woman. The lyrics are funny, but there's a core of sadness to them. What y'all are doing is matching the rhythm with the emotion." He strummed the guitar, fingers plucking over the strings. "How about if we play against them, make it up-tempo? Let the audience find the sorrow in the song while they're dancing." Establishing a fast honky-tonk beat, he gestured for the rhythm guitar, bass, and drums to follow along. Once they had, he started playing the melody and nodded to Jessica to sing.

The addition of the bouncy beat underscored the latent melancholy in the song. Alanna was watching him with open-mouthed surprise.

A corner of his mouth tilted up. "Cowboy's got to do something when he's herding cattle on the range with nothing but his horse and his hat for company." *Damn it.* He shouldn't be talking to her as though they were friends.

"Guess so."

He directed his attention to the pretty blonde singer. "What do you think?" Once he had been the fixer and not just for marketing. He'd gone from fast-rising executive to pariah in a matter of months and never recovered.

Jessica nodded.

He handed the guitar back to the guitarist and motioned to the sound engineer. "Let's hear the rest of it while I'm here, give me some ideas."

When they were done, they retreated to the lounge while the musicians continued their recording. Half-eaten pizzas and fruit and vegetable platters were scattered on the tables. The upholstered sofa had threads showing at the arms. An old-style arcade game sat in the corner, its lights blinking. A bar provided refreshments, both alcoholic and nonalcoholic.

Dirk stood, tapping his chin as he gathered his thoughts. They had listened to the recorded tracks twice.

"Much as I hate to say it, I think we got to go with 'Susan' for the first release," he said. "We risk alienating country fans with a crossover, but it's the best one on the album."

"Maybe. That's not our call to make. I'll talk to her manager—unless you want to do it." Ally's voice was hesitant, as if she wasn't quite sure of his suggestion.

He considered his options. He was not her boss, but he was above her within the company. Before he arrived, she likely had direct access to Gordon. Now he was the layer in between.

He remembered a time before he climbed up the corporate ladder when his ideas would either have been ignored or co-opted by his bosses. He might be persona non grata throughout much of the industry, but that didn't mean he couldn't be a decent human being. "Nah. You got this. You know her better than I do. It would be foolish for me to step in and disrupt things now."

She chewed on her upper lip but didn't meet his gaze. "Okay. I can do that. Thanks, Dirk." Hurt dashed across her face before she stilled it into a neutral, composed façade.

He whuffed out a breath, understanding her expression was a false front. He hadn't lived with his wife for ten years without knowing how to read people. "I bet you could grab him at the marketing meeting on Monday mornings. That way he'd have to listen."

She gave him a tiny smile. The green room was empty although he could hear the sounds of the band down the hall. The room shrank in size, reminding Dirk how near she was.

Time to go.

"I could eat a horse. Let's grab some chow before we go back."

"Sure. What are you in the mood for? There's pretty much everything around here." She started ticking them off on her fingers. "Italian, Indian, Mexican, Chinese, Japanese?" She laughed as he made a face at the last one. "Sorry. You don't like Japanese. I have a place in mind. We're not far."

Chapter Four

Ally hoped he liked her choice. When she'd first been introduced to the restaurant, she'd been starting out in the business but now made it a point to try and come whenever she was nearby.

Roscoe's House of Chicken N' Waffles was a restaurant on Gower Street in the heart of Hollywood, just north of Sunset. The needle on top of the Capitol Records building could be glimpsed through buildings in the distance. The Sunset Gower studios with their art deco lettering were just down the street. The Hollywood Hills loomed behind them, if a person faced north.

The restaurant itself had a simple, brown-painted front and a sign with a picture of a dancing chicken overhead. Haphazard graffiti marred some of the storefronts, and trash bounced along the edges of the street. Muted winter sunshine cast a golden glow across the streets and buildings.

Roscoe's boasted down-home Southern fare, consisting of fried chicken with sides such as grits, macaroni and cheese, as well as their famous waffles. The restaurant was crowded at lunchtime with an eclectic mix of clientele, from tourists to local businesspeople.

The restaurant was a study in two separate parts. One was the original side, and one was a larger addition. The older side was cozy with a raised step after they entered. Plain brown tables and wooden chairs with curving open backs were wedged close.

The table that Dirk and Ally sat at was next to a wall with slanted, dark wood paneling. Artwork and photos were strewn across the walls.

Dirk had to adjust his legs so they were splayed out on either side of Ally when they were seated. He was like an adult on a kid-sized bike.

The smell of fried chicken mixed with less identifiable odors permeated the air. "It's probably not authentic," she said, "but I hope you like it." It shouldn't matter, yet it did. *Damn it.*

He rewarded her with a smile that sent a bolt of sensation through her spine.

"I am sure I will. Thank you. Fried chicken and grits are just what a Southern boy needs to feel at home."

He opened his mouth to say something to her, then went so still he could have been carved of stone. Following his gaze, she saw a man a few years older than Dirk, with the same slightly weathered skin of outdoor living. A brown Stetson was on his head, with jeans and a denim shirt completing the outfit. The glare he was giving Dirk was so malevolent she shivered. He was standing with a group by a curio cabinet studded with Roscoe's souvenirs at the front of the restaurant. One of the people she recognized as Ryder Bingham, an artist whose album had recently been certified platinum.

She turned back to Dirk. His lips had flattened to a thin line, and harsh grooves cut next to his eyes and down his face before they disappeared under the goatee.

"Heard you landed at Shatter Sound," the shorter

man said, his arms folded and his face in profile to Ally. He was a short man, maybe her height at best, with thick brown hair shot with gray and a close-cropped beard. He also had a drawl that was different somehow than Dirk's but clearly Southern. "Should have done the smart thing and stayed away." The dim light from the window touched his shoulders, matching the sliver that landed across Dirk's chest.

"You should know, Marlon," Dirk said, his voice cold, body rigid, his hands clasping and unclasping on the table. "I never did learn my lessons easy." He focused on her. "Marlon works at Earthy Cry Records. Marlon, Alanna Wilson."

"Ma'am." Marlon lifted his hat. "You're at his new the label. Watch this boy like a hawk, or he'll take you too." He shot Dirk a cold glance, turned his back on them, and walked away, rejoining his group. When the host came to seat them, Marlon pointed out Dirk, then to a table in the corner where they wouldn't have to make eye contact with the offending duo seated in the older section.

As they passed through the tiny restaurant, Ryder separated from the group and headed for Dirk.

"Hey, hoss," Ryder said, hovering in front of their table.

"Hey, bud," Dirk returned. "Didn't realize you were in town. Ryder, meet Alanna Wilson."

She accepted the hand he extended.

He shook her hand with a smile tugging on his lips. "I'm Ryder Bingham."

He was a big man too, not as big as Dirk, but probably six feet three. He was a good-looking man in a more traditional way than Dirk, with a mane of brown hair and whiskey-colored amber eyes.

Marlon glared at the three of them, his stare evident even from a distance.

"Nice to meet you, Ryder." She dredged up any news articles she could recall into her mind. "Congratulations on going platinum."

He inclined his head in thanks.

"You better get back to Marl before he skins you alive. Give me a call if you have time."

"Will do." Ryder waved a hand in farewell and left.

Ally turned to watch Ryder retreat to the table in the far corner by the front door. Marlon gave Dirk another cold stare, then turned away, his back to the couple.

"I'm sorry," she said. "This is a popular spot. Lots of studio and music folks come here."

Dirk shook his head at her words. "Not your fault, darlin'."

"So how…" Her voice trailed off. Dirk had come cheap for a reason. Gordon might have put them all at risk hiring someone the industry didn't trust. Maybe her future job would be easier to get than she thought.

She ignored the awareness that was telling her to try and seduce him. That was something that would never—ever—happen.

"Marlon and I go back ten years. He took me on at the label. Guess you could call him my mentor. We were friends. Once. That was before he accused me of treachery and got me fired." Regret laced his tone, the drawl thickening until she could barely understand him. A tremor rolled through his big body as he half turned away from her, showing her only his hard-etched profile, the ponytail at the back of his head hitting the bones of his neck.

"He...um..." Rumors swirled through her mind. "They said you purposely blew a big campaign. They never said why."

She detected no humor in the harsh bark that served for a laugh, his body jerking with the noise.

"I know what they say, Alanna. I can say I had nothing to do with it all I want, but the truth is it happened on my watch, so I am responsible. Buck stops with me, and I took the fall." His baritone was rough. He faced her again, fingers outstretched on the table. He yanked his legs away from her and started to get up, bumping his knees on the underside of the table before freeing them. "I was an idiot to come here."

She couldn't tell if he meant Roscoe's or Los Angeles in general—or both. The scrape on the floor was loud, even with the conversations in the room. His large body was half in and half out of the chair, long torso casting a shadow across them. The table rocked with his jerky movements, and the customer behind him started in surprise.

Ryder's head came up at Dirk's sudden movement. The tables around them had fallen silent, but she shoved that awareness to the back of her mind. Letting him go would be smarter.

His face was ashen, lips thinned to mere slashes. His teeth were set, and a muscle jumped in the back of his jaw. Even in the dim light, she could tell that his pupils were nothing but pinpoints. Hunched shoulders and rigid elbows spoke to a tension in his body that would have broken a lesser man.

The twisting of her heart was familiar, as much as Ally wanted to deny what she was feeling. This man who was an obstacle not only in the very real physical sense, but more importantly, to her career, was also a human being. She could be a friend, no matter what the future held. He was gruff, scared, and so very alone.

"Unless you're planning on standing me up for lunch," she said, digging deep to find a balance of asperity and pleading, "would you please sit back down?"

After a long beat he sat, sliding the chair forward with his foot until he could brace his body in it again, his gaze never leaving hers.

She leaned over so only he could hear her words. Gratefully she became aware that the babble of conversation around them had resumed. Ryder turned his attention back to the speaking Marlon.

"I can be a fool—that is for sure." She longed to stroke her hands over his back and soothe him. The tension hadn't left him, as the steely grip of his fingers on the table showed. "It's too early to tell where this particular situation falls on the scale of idiocy. We've got a job to do together. Gordon's orders. Relax. The chicken here is great." She hoped the dim light of the restaurant would cover the guilty heat on her cheeks. It wouldn't change what she was set to do, but she could defer that for the moment. The day of reckoning would come, but not today.

Ally waited. Finally, he relaxed, the color coming back to his face. Electricity poured off him, making her heart pound. Excitement flared across her nerve endings.

"Besides," she continued, "I believe we have a football game to watch this weekend. You're still in, right?"

"I got an idea," he said finally.

The return of his normal amused drawl relieved her.

He splayed out again, legs alongside her own and arms folded across his chest. "How every time the Falcons score a touchdown you have to chant 'Dirty Birds.' "

"Hmm. Only if you will promise that when New England wins the Super Bowl, you have to wear a Patriots jersey to work."

His snort of laughter almost made her giggle. "It's a deal."

****

Their lunch came, and Dirk stared at the plate that held three pieces of brown battered chicken, red beans, rice with gravy, and cornbread. A separate white bowl had grits, something Alanna said she'd never tried before.

He picked up a piece of chicken, although his pleasure at the outing had faded. The drumstick was still warm from the fryer, its skin a crispy golden brown. Marlon's enmity brought back those last months in Nashville. He should have known something similar would happen in Los Angeles eventually. The altercation didn't take away from his plan. He had to stick to that and not get distracted. By anything—or anyone.

Ally tapped her plate. He turned his head up to hers and focused on the blonde across the table from him. A woman he found much too compelling.

"If you'd rather not stay, we can get this to go. The subway is close by, and there's a park above it. We could go sit on a bench and eat."

A short grunt escaped him. Getting used to this woman would be too easy. She'd offered him more comfort than anyone had in years. He fought the temptation to take it and see where else he could press his advantage.

"Naw, I'll be fine. This is nothing. You weren't in Nashville. It can be a real small town. That's mighty decent of you, though."

Her face turned. "Small towns. They're not always what they're supposed to be, are they?"

A buried pain moved across her face, twisting her features like a giant stone that sat on her soul. Her mouth turned down. For a minute, the pain on her face was so intense it shook him to his core. His fingers twitched with the longing to cover hers.

She seemed to become aware of his scrutiny because she smiled, poking at her bowl with a desultory motion. He could no longer detect any of the sorrow.

Or the smile.

"Guess I don't have to worry about that here. Small towns, that is," he said. With that he picked up the drumstick and bit into it. The chicken was surprisingly tender, the flaky batter crisp on his tongue, and the meat juicy. "Good chicken."

"I think so. I'm glad you agree." She stared at the white bowl that contained the grits he'd insisted she order.

He gestured with his chin. "Try your grits."

"They look like cream of wheat."

He grinned, pleasure sliding through him at being able to show her something new. He refused to put a label on what that sensation meant. "Don't taste like them, though. Trust me, Alanna. You will not be sorry."

Picking up her spoon, she tentatively dipped it into the bowl of white creamed hominy laced with so much butter it pooled in melted yellow ponds across the top of the grits. He waited as she took the spoon and pressed it to the tip of her tongue.

"Whoa. I wasn't expecting that. They taste like corn meal and butter mixed together. Like savory cream of wheat. I like them," she declared.

His body surged at the sight of her pink tongue. He shifted, fighting a sudden need to taste that mouth with his own. His hands gripped the drumstick, nearly snapping it in half, as he fought the urge to lean over and kiss her.

All the reasons he couldn't do anything of the sort settled his libido. He might be as hard as stone around Alanna, but he had nothing to offer her. He was tainted, his reputation destroyed. He was no longer the rising star of the marketing world, able to fix a band with his innovative campaigns. One mistake under his watch had ensured that there would be no happily ever after with Dirk. He couldn't offer any woman, especially this one, a white picket fence and kids laughing in the yard. Not yet. Not while things were the way they were. Not when she was there to spy on him and take the job owed to her at the same time.

The problem was he liked her. He liked her quick wit, her ready comebacks, her quiet generosity to friends and strangers. He liked the way she got things done without broadcasting her accomplishments. She'd taken him on and taken him in, smiling at the man who stepped in between her and the next job title, a man whose reputation should have made him a nonstarter. This gift horse had a lot of issues.

"Wow," she continued. "They're good." She dipped the spoon in again and came away with a generous helping.

"Told you." Having dispatched the drumstick, he turned to the grits next, mixing the butter in, then taking a spoonful of his own portion and tasting them. "They are good. Not as good as Mama's, but better than I expected."

They ate in silence for a minute. He didn't want to be easy in her company, but the companionable silence was familiar, like he'd known her for years.

"Ryder seems like he's still your friend."

Time for the fishing expedition. He'd been expecting it, and it hardened his resolve. He was a fool to let this one close. "He didn't buy into the BS the company peddled at the time we parted ways. I always did like Ryder."

"Good. We should always be allowed to make up our own minds about people. How do you know each other?"

He pushed his plate away from him and leaned back in the tiny chair that was way too small for his massive frame. "He's an Earthy Cry artist. I did his first two albums back when I was the next marketing genius. Remember the song 'Call My Name'?"

She pointed to herself, a wry smile twisting her face. "Rock and roller here, remember? Country and I are not old friends."

He barked out something that might have been laughter before cutting it short, unwilling to let her see how charmed he was by her. "The tune was off the first album. It didn't smash through but charted enough to get him signed to a second deal. I did the campaign for it, and we hit it off. Started hanging out—mostly pool and beer buddy stuff. After Earthy Cry dumped me, Ryder called me up, said if he could do anything to help, to let him know. Crazy who shows up when the chips are down."

"I'm going to download all Ryder's albums."

He couldn't suppress his grin. "Ryder had a rough life as a kid. He understands how things can get messed up. He said he didn't believe the crap they were peddling."

"There you go. Los Angeles is a city of second chances."

"Yes…" Something in her demeanor stilled his words. He thought back to the way her face changed when she spoke about small towns. Whatever he was about to say died within him. Women were different than guys. Guys were big and strong and could hold their own. Women were fragile, breakable, and to be protected.

Ally wasn't frail. She was solid, her tall, lush form reassuring him that she wouldn't snap easily. He watched her as she ate her own drumstick, biting it with neat nips of her teeth.

"I like a woman who isn't afraid of food," he said.

Her mouth twisted before she smiled again. Once again that gesture came nowhere near her eyes.

"Are you kidding? Roscoe's has the best fried chicken in town. I'm not going to sit here and eat it with a knife and fork or pick at it, pretending that my mouth isn't watering."

His bark of laughter was short. "Then let's get to it."

"Right. We should get back anyway. We've got

work to do."

Whatever she'd actually been about to say vanished. Dirk wished he didn't wonder what that was.

Chapter Five

"It ain't Georgia, but I'm getting used to it."

Dirk leaned against the plate glass window, gazing out over the Burbank skyline and into the Hollywood Hills. What he wouldn't give for the rolling green hills and lush vegetation of his Georgia hometown. A blast of homesickness took him before he realized his brother was still talking.

"What's that again?"

"I said do they run around in bikinis on the streets?"

Greg's Georgia accent was thicker than Dirk's, who had spent several months losing his drawl so he could be understood to his business counterparts.

"Nah. They wear normal clothes. Some folks got crazy ideas of fashion here, but that's in some of the more—what do they call it?—avant-garde parts of town. There's shit they wouldn't be caught dead wearing in Nashville, not without getting laughed at. Most folks here dress all right. Different than back home, but not too weird."

Greg chuckled, a sound that reminded Dirk of their father. Longing, not just for the town in Georgia where they were raised, but for his family and his former way of life, swam within him. He stared out the window, not seeing the people on the sidewalk several floors below.

"Don't go getting citified, little bro."

"Y'all said that to me when I moved to Nashville. I ain't your little bro. I got four inches on you."

His brother's snicker made the longing for the town he grew up in intensify. He couldn't walk away yet. Not without destroying everything he was rebuilding. It sure was tempting, though. He should get out before he got in any deeper. Before he allowed his attraction for a woman he should not look at twice take him over.

"You're two years younger than me. You'll always be that. Ain't nothing you can do to change it."

His body moved with the grunt of amusement that rolled through him. Old family jokes never got old. "I can still whup you ten ways from Sunday. I wish I were there. This place is not for me."

Even as he said it, a vision of Alanna swam into his mind. The way she took it in stride when Marlon went for him at Roscoe's warmed him in a way he hadn't expected. He had no illusions as to what she was up to, yet she still offered sympathy. No, Los Angeles wasn't for him. The woman could be.

Who was he kidding? This was goddamn Los Angeles. She was likely as treacherous as the rest and just better at hiding it. He should be wary of her and not wondering what it would be like to kiss her. Or more than just a smooch. He was a lunatic to be thinking such thoughts. Even if he hadn't been in her way in her climb up the corporate ladder, he was fully aware that she was watching him. Hell, he would be too if the situations were reversed.

"Are you going to come home soon? Mama has been asking." Greg's voice held no recrimination, just curiosity.

Dirk chuckled. "She's been taught how to work the video conferencing. She doesn't need to use my older brother as a message board. I'll call her. I doubt I can get away, but I'll see what I can do. I got to go. Kiss Maisie and the kids for me."

He hung up and put his cell down. It had gotten dark as they talked. The lights came on, giving the night a sparkling glow. At home there might be snow or a sheen of ice that made everything bright, but here the colors were brown or browner.

This city would never accept him. He was always going to be an out-of-place Southerner in a foreign city. Then again, Alanna said Los Angeles was a good place to start over.

Maybe she was right.

His direct messages dinged, and he focused on his computer. He still had work to do and should be paying attention to that instead of the woman who was getting under his skin. The future held nothing for Dirk and some Los Angeles female, no matter how sexy he found her. She believed her loose-fitting clothes hid her form, but she was wrong. Her lush curves were apparent despite the disguise. He ached to touch them to determine if they were as soft as he hoped.

He had no business thinking about any of that. A year, maybe two at the most, and his reputation would be as repaired as possible. Then he could return home. Things would never be the same, but it would be enough. Even now he burned to be home, back east with the rolling hills and lush greenery. Not here where rain was a distant memory and palm trees were the order of the day.

He wouldn't stay here forever, no matter the

woman who had started to haunt his nightly fantasies. She was the best reason not to consider a place like this home. He had no business dreaming of what life would be like with a gal like her.

He needed to get out of there. He had worked well past quitting time. He should not do what was uppermost in his mind, which was seek out Alanna and find out her plans for the weekend.

That was not what he should do. He had to go before he did something he would regret. Dirk packed up his belongings, grabbed for his hat, and headed out the door.

He'd get some takeout on the way home and try to forget the color of Alanna's eyes.

****

Ally needed to talk to someone. Maybe Terri. She'd let Terri drift out of her life, but now she wondered why she had done that. Terri knew what it was like to get wrapped up in a guy. She would understand.

Maybe later. Terri might not comprehend how Ally was even contemplating a man from the South. She understood Southerners about as well as Ally did—that was to say, not at all.

Gordon knocked on her office door and poked his head in. "Got a minute?"

She waved him inside. "What's up?" She tried to keep her voice professional. This man had taken her job from her, given it to a man he didn't trust, and then asked her to spy. She should have said no, but she wanted that promotion. Had earned it. She would get it, and then…she had no idea. In this time of collapsing labels, jobs were hard to come by. Dirk was a great example. She was sure that his job aspirations had not included a move to California.

"How is it going with Jess? Have you and Dirk come up with a campaign strategy?"

"We're working on it. I took him down to the studio to meet Jess and listen to the tracks. It gave him some ideas." She had given Gordon her concepts before, and he'd pushed them aside. Maybe Dirk could get them through.

"I heard about that. Then afterward. They're calling it the shootout at the Roscoe's Corral in the office."

Despite her resentment, she managed a smile. "No guns were drawn, I assure you. The rumors have blown it out of proportion. He generates controversy, but you knew that going in."

"Yeah." He tapped Ally's desk, directing her attention. "Have you learned anything? What do you think? I can count on you to give me the real deal. It's early days, but a general impression."

She took in a breath and then let it out. She needed to think long-term and be strategic. "He's good. He's got decent ideas. We're still working through them."

"That's not what I'm asking about." He tapped her desk again. "What do you think about the…rest of it?"

She longed to scream, "If you don't trust him, why did you hire him?" She kept those words unspoken. She would prove herself, even if it took longer than it should have.

"I can't tell. He hasn't done anything to raise eyebrows except be Dirk, but that's enough. As you said, the shootout at the Roscoe's Corral. He comes with a ton of baggage. In terms of the company, it's too soon to tell. I assume you're keeping him away from the finances."

"Of course." Gordon rose and glanced around her office. "Keep it up. You can never tell what might happen if you play your cards right."

When he left, she spun in her chair. The carrot he was dangling in front of her was apparent. Like the stupid mule she was, she would grab at it.

The whole thing wasn't fair at all.

She packed up, unable to take another minute in the office. The weekend loomed in front of her with its promise of free time. She had work she could do, of course, but not this night. Right now, she just wanted to get out of there and head home.

Ally didn't want to see Dirk. She did want to see him. Her emotions rolled inside her like spiky balls, scoring her with their barbs.

The tall figure heading for his car was unmistakably Dirk. Nobody was that big or wore that sort of hat except him. If she kept to the shadows, he wouldn't see her. Letting him slip into the night would be smarter.

"Hey, Dirk, wait up! Where you off to in such a hurry?" Ally hoped her voice carried to his ears and waited to see what he would do.

He hesitated, and she wondered what he was going to say. She didn't know what made him so tense, but he was agitated. She fought the sympathy that welled up inside her.

"I'm going home. I've got a hot date with a TV and a goddamn efficiency apartment," he growled, hooding his eyes with his cowboy hat. "Maybe the internet if I'm feeling frisky. Don't worry about me, Alanna. It's

Friday. I'm sure your friends are waiting for you."

The call of voices saying goodbye echoed through the structure as employees went to their cars. The sun set early this time of year, and feeble light from the parking-structure lamps cast them into shadow, silhouetted on the concrete. A breeze swirled around them, lifting the bottom of his duster and catching the edges of her hair.

"I'm not up for drinks," she said. She took a step toward him and watched to see if he would retreat, breathing out a sigh of relief when he didn't. It shouldn't matter to her. He was just a job. A man in her way.

"Damn it, Alanna." He jerked his arms in a downward motion. "Work is over. You don't owe me anything."

She should let him go home. She should stop this ridiculous behavior. The office was buzzing about the amount of time she spent with Dirk. Even recognizing that she had a job to do—one Gordon handed her—didn't help. A smart woman would have gone out with the gang, had a few cocktails, and hung out. If she lost the confidence of her co-workers, it wouldn't matter if she got the promotion when Dirk left. The damage would be done.

"I don't. You're right about that. Nonetheless, here I am."

He took a deep breath, lifting his hat and adjusting it before he focused on her again.

"You don't think you're fooling anyone with that hat thing, do you? It's a stall tactic."

Dirk's startled glance made a quick smile flit across her face.

"It's not a stall tactic so much as a nervous habit," he admitted. "Gives me something to do with my hands. There's no need for this. Leave me be. I'll be fine."

She took another step forward, and they were face-to-face. His lips were pressed together, distorting the goatee. The heat of his body cut through the air like electricity. She fought not to hug this giant of a man until the lines of his face eased and the tension left his body.

"Whether you are or not is up for debate. What if I said I didn't want to let you be?"

Breath exploded out of his lungs in a shaky laugh. "Woman, you have a hell of a way with words."

The lines bracketing his mouth eased until his lips were no longer so thin.

"I'd rather spend tonight swapping stories than talking about how to make our artists famous. Today is Friday. I'm done talking business. We could get some takeout and go back to my place. I've got beer, and we could watch movies or cartoons or something."

"You don't have any Dixie, do you?"

Ally stared at him without comprehension. Then he grinned, and she understood she was being teased. A surge of pleasure ran through her. This was going to have to stop.

Later.

"Beer," he amended, taking off his hat and adjusting it again.

"There's a beer called Dixie?" She tried to keep her tone neutral.

"I'm funning you. I prefer Miller. Genuine Draft, if it makes a difference. The cartoons—are they Looney

Tunes?"

" 'Course!" She was unable to help a flash of a grin. He would hear the mimicry in her voice. "I'm not into the Simpsons or SpongeBob or anime. Give me Wile E. Coyote and the Roadrunner any day of the week. Oh, and Marvin the Martian and Bugs Bunny naturally."

"No Daffy Duck?"

She waved her hand in dismissal. "Nah."

"Good. Me either. All right, you talked me into it. Let's stop at my crap place first so I can change."

****

The minute they entered her house, she kicked off her shoes and went to the kitchen to get supplies. "Hey, do you mind starting a fire?" She raised her voice to be heard in the next room. "Everything is right there. All you have to do is get the kindling and the logs started."

"Sure thing."

She thought about pouring herself a stiff belt of vodka but was afraid if she did, she might drink too much, then crawl on his lap and beg him to kiss her. Forcing herself to pour one shot, and one shot only, she opened his beer.

"I've got the Bugs Bunny/Roadrunner movie on DVD if you're in the mood for Looney Tunes," she continued. "It's in the video cabinet on the right wall near the fireplace."

His heavy tread was loud, the staccato thump of cowboy boots on hardwood echoing. Oh God, they were in her house, and they were alone. Swallowing hard against the surge of desire that idea brought, she arranged their dinners on a tray—burgers and fries for him and a Chinese chicken salad for her—then reentered the living room.

He was standing in front of the video cabinet when she walked in, the red glow of a new fire visible in the fireplace. His duster was draped across one of the barstools. The sleeveless white shirt he'd changed into was a slash of light in the dimly lit room, its creamy paleness a nice contrast to his tanned skin. Old faded jeans curved around his body, and a cap that said "Ryder" was on his head.

"Streaming would be easier."

She used her shoulder to nudge toward the cabinet. "Probably. We can check that too if you'd rather. They don't always have what I am in the mood for, so I keep my DVDs."

"Guess that makes sense. You're old school. I like it. Don't you like any one genre?" He gestured to the video cabinet. "There's a little bit of everything in here."

Setting the tray down on the coffee table, she joined him at the alphabetized grouping of DVDs. Handing him the beer, she spoke. "Nope. I am eclectic as heck." She took out two DVDs, *Die Hard* and *Casablanca*, and showed them to him. "I love both these movies, for different reasons. Why do I need to choose? Why should anyone choose? Entertainment is entertainment. Why is it we stick to preset boundaries?" She replaced them in the cabinet, aware that her voice had taken on that defensive quality again.

Cartoons, Ally? You must be kidding.

"Sure," he agreed. "Otherwise, all I'd be allowed to watch is *Blue Collar TV.*"

When she laughed, his shoulders went down. Whether he was relaxing because of her or because the week was over, she wasn't sure, but she hugged the victory to herself like a talisman.

This madness had to stop. She really, really didn't want to like him.

He took the Bugs Bunny/Roadrunner DVD from its spot and handed it to Ally. "I think we both could use a good laugh."

They talked for over an hour before starting the DVD. She learned that he had been a business major. He was from Georgia. His parents had been married for forty-five years, and he was the younger of two brothers.

She told him pieces of her past. What her relationship with her younger sister was like. How their parents' divorce, albeit a civilized one as those things went, had impacted both of them. The challenges she faced moving out to Los Angeles to go to college. How she had lucked into her first job at a management company where a boss had trusted her enough to let her try her hand at assistant manager. Then manager. How everything had gone from there.

They dodged the giant topics, the ones that would shatter this artificial peace and make a mockery of this new friendship. She was afraid that it wouldn't matter to her if he'd told her he committed the crimes he was accused of. This peaceful time was the perfect opportunity to snoop and get answers. Yet she didn't.

When they finally ran out of topics—and food—she made popcorn. They had to either watch the movie or...she wouldn't think about that. Either that or pounce on the gorgeous man in her living room.

As she got ready to insert the DVD in the player, she noted in the reflection of the TV that Dirk groaned, flexing his cowboy-boot-shod feet.

She turned back to point at his feet. "Take them off."

He tilted his head, giving her an uncomprehending stare.

"Take them off," she repeated. "I don't know how you've stood it for this long. I did." She raised one foot to show him her naked toes. "Took them off, that is."

They weren't very pretty feet. The toes were bare of polish. They were too wide and too long to be the stuff of fetishists' wet dreams. Nevertheless, they were solid and would withstand much abuse in the years to come.

"You ever wear nail polish?"

She flushed at the myriad ways in which she was not feminine. She wished she could be, full of clouds of expensive perfume, redolent with the aura of sheer femininity. She was just Ally, a former tomboy, not elegant even in her best costumes.

"Not very often," she admitted. "Only for special occasions. I tend to pick at it until it starts peeling off."

Dirk chuckled, a rich bayou sound. "Good. I don't like all that stuff."

She tried to control her annoyance. This man got to her, making her usual defenses tough to maintain. Would it kill him to tell her how gorgeous she was? She'd gotten used to casual insults from others, but from this man, it stung.

Pursing her lips, she inclined her head to one side. "In all honesty, Dirk, I'm not sure how I'm supposed to take that."

He met her gaze, his brow furrowing.

She had an urge to get up and walk out of the

room. She waited, taking deep breaths to stop from revealing her emotions. She was fighting the hurt that welled up inside her, the pain that she was being mocked surging within her. Maybe Dirk wasn't like that—but maybe he was. She had already proven she was a lousy judge of character.

It shouldn't matter.

Unfortunately, it did.

Chapter Six

Damn it. Dirk was out of the practice of talking to women. Women liked sweet talk and comfortable social lies. Not that a man liked them because they didn't drape themselves in all that crap.

Ally held up her hand. "No need to sugarcoat it, Dirk, just tell me."

He liked that she was sturdy, but he didn't have the words to say it right. That she was the type who wouldn't mind getting dirty. That she wouldn't hold her nose in the air if she had to muck out a stall or need a lot of fancy makeup or perfume to adorn her.

A woman didn't need to hear those things. That wasn't what they longed to be told.

He stated it anyway. She'd asked for honesty, and he gave it to her.

To his surprise, she laughed when he finished.

"Tomboy." Her face held no trace of wounded vanity. If anything, she seemed amused. "I've always been a tomboy."

Sexiest tomboy I ever saw.

"Darlin', most tomboys ain't built like you."

She bit the pad of her right thumb, then worried the edge of the nail with her teeth. "I was small up until eighth grade."

The words were simple, but the flare of pain that flashed across her face wasn't. That same hand came up

65

and played over the faint scars around her right eye in an absentminded gesture.

Damn it. He was itching to learn what put that horrible vulnerable pain on her soul. To cover the urge to pull her into his arms, he yanked his boots off one at a time, letting them fall as he removed them. The sudden easing in the pinching of his feet made him sigh in relief.

She turned to the DVD player and pressed play. "Time to watch Bugs and Road Runner, I think."

They watched the entire movie with its various segments, discussing their differences about Porky Pig and whether or not "What's Opera Doc" was the best skit, or the Road Runner ones were better.

Ally then popped in a DVD of Pink Panther cartoons, and they stretched out, one to either side of her sectional couch. He almost fit, flexing his knees to accommodate his large frame.

They both agreed that nothing was cooler than the Pink Panther.

Without being aware of the bone-deep weariness in him or even that he was tired, he fell asleep.

The scent of coffee nudged Dirk awake. A sense of peace filled him, something he hadn't experienced for a long time.

Then he started, coming to his senses in a room that was familiar to him but not his bedroom.

Fire.

Cartoons.

Alanna.

He was in Alanna's living room. On her couch. A blanket was tucked around him, and his cap was resting toward him on the coffee table.

A hint of morning light slanted across her blinds.

Stretching, he tried to guess the time. Eight or so, he hazarded. He focused on the DVD player in front of him in the entertainment unit. *8:17.*

The morning hours were used to get chores done before the day began. Except he had no chores to do in an efficiency apartment.

Soft singing came from the kitchen.

He had fallen asleep on Alanna. He should have been embarrassed but instead felt alive.

Smoothing his hair into place, he settled the cap over his head. With quiet movements, he padded toward the kitchen.

Clad in burgundy-colored, cotton drawstring pants and a white tank, Ally had her back to him as she washed dishes in the sink. Her hair had been brushed but was still kinked in that way sleep did. The top outlined her body, curving around her shoulders and down to her tapered waist. The pants were loose and, as with many of her clothes, designed to conceal rather than reveal. The outline of her strong thighs was still visible under the cloth. *Wow.* He liked nice, high, round butts, and hers fit the bill to a T.

Straining to figure out what song she was singing to herself, he pegged it as "What a Fool Believes" by the Doobie Brothers. A slow grin played over his face.

Arms crossed, he leaned on the doorframe to the kitchen. "Don't you ever wear shoes?" he asked with an amused drawl.

She spun, sponge in her hand. The force of her spin made water spray across her shirt and onto the floor. The water began seeping in across the side of one of her breasts.

Then those glorious lips parted over a smile. One that made it to her eyes. "You could teach a cat about stealth. Good morning to you too." Setting the sponge down, she rinsed off her hands, then removed a dishtowel from a hook that had a smiling, dancing pig on it. The theme carried through to additional towels draped in the stove handle.

"Not if I can help it," she continued, placing the towel back in a nearby ring. "Hate the things. Kick them off first chance I get. Even in winter, unless my feet are blocks of ice, shoes don't exist when I'm home." She retrieved two plain coffee cups from a nearby cabinet from it. "The siren lure of my couch has claimed an additional victim. Sleep well?"

"Your couch famous for its soporific qualities?"

If she was startled at his use of the four-syllable word, she gave no sign of it. Grinning at him, she moved past to the coffee maker in the dining room. He pressed himself back against the door opening to try and give her room, but the swell of her large breast grazed his chest anyway. The wetness of her tank top riveted his attention, and he could make out a plain white bra underneath the shirt. The desire to bend down and taste those breasts with his tongue overwhelmed him for a minute. He swore under his breath, counting backward from a hundred to bring his body back under control.

"Big time. I've fallen asleep on it more times than I can count. How do you take your coffee?" she asked.

"Black."

"Me too." She poured the coffee and handed the mug to him.

"For real?" He raised an eyebrow.

"Yeah, why?"

He'd stepped in it somehow but couldn't figure out what had happened. "Dunno. You just seem more like the type to enjoy the sweet things in life."

The sudden bleakness came and went, but he noted it before she shut down, presenting him with a bland countenance.

"Not like that, Alanna." Her mulish appearance told him all that had done was make her shut down further. He shouldn't care. He should change the subject. Instead, he waited for her to answer, trying to ignore the shaft of pain that lanced through him that he'd caused her hurt.

****

Ally took a deep breath. She shouldn't take her insecurities out on Dirk. With a conscious effort, she relaxed her shoulders and turned her face up to meet his gaze.

"You have to understand I was a size eighteen before I understood I had to make changes if I had any hope of slimming down. Cutting out cream and sugar eliminated fifty calories per cup. It may not be much, but every bit helped."

She met his penetrating green gaze. "At first I hated it. The taste was so bitter before I discovered French Roast and dark blends. Their aromatic taste made it palatable. This stuff is Jamaica Blue Mountain Coffee, probably the finest in the world. Try it."

"Nothing wrong with an eighteen. I bet you were gorgeous," he murmured. He tried the brew, keeping eye contact as he did so.

She could see by the way his smile tilted up that he appreciated the coffee. The idea that she'd done something good made her insides flip over.

Damn it.

"I bet I wasn't."

"Bet you were." His mouth twitched with suppressed amusement.

"Wasn't."

"Was."

Standing there in bare feet in her dining room, she had an ease in his presence that was unlike anything she'd experienced before.

"I've got the pictures to prove I wasn't." Setting the cup down, she gestured for Dirk to follow her.

The spare room was sparse, three walls lined with bookshelves. A desk with a sleek, new computer faced the window. The big willow tree that was in the back of her front yard was visible through thin burgundy curtains. A light breeze rippled the curtains through the open window. An area rug broke the lines of the hardwood floor.

The makeshift shelves weren't professional, and it showed. She'd needed somewhere to put her book collection and had nobody to help. She'd decided to build them. Armed with a hammer, wood cut from the local hardware store, and a level, she'd created them from scratch. They might not be professional, but she had stained them all in a dark oak color so they all matched. She had a fair inkling of what he beheld. Half-assed bookshelves and books. A mixture of hardcover and paperback, her collection was all over the map. As with her DVDs, she didn't stick to any particular genre. Classics, romance, horror, science fiction, as well as many different categories of nonfiction were all present. The books were categorized by genre, then alphabetized by author and title.

His grin was infectious. For any man to look this good in the morning ought to be illegal. There should be a law prohibiting any man from being that big, with eyes that vibrant, lips that kissable, hair that gorgeous, and a body that made a woman feel protected—safe.

"Hmm." He glanced around the room. "You like to read?"

"Nope." She hoped the tilt to her lips let him recognize she was kidding. "They're decoration."

Grinning, he examined the books closer. "Hillerman?"

She recalled the author's moody, complex mysteries set in the West, with two Native American heroes named Joe Leaphorn and Jim Chee.

"Sure. He's great. I think Joe Leaphorn is one of the finest drawn characters in modern history."

Dirk's grin widened. "I've got all of them in first edition hardcover in storage at home. Even got a signed one. Belinda got it for me one year for my birthday."

"Really?" She hoped her surprise didn't show as badly as she suspected it did. "I guess I had you pegged as a Clive Cussler or W.E.B. Griffin fan."

He laughed, a hearty sound that evoked muggy summer days thick with the scent of magnolias and pine. The sorts that were made for slow lovemaking, naked, sweaty bodies sliding over each other...

Stop. It. Ally.

"Cussler's main character is named Dirk. It'd be weird to see my name every few sentences."

She chuckled. "I never thought of it that way." She'd done it again. She'd assumed based on his appearance, and his background, that he would have certain tastes. Instead, he'd once again surprised her by his interest in a multifaceted writer like Tony Hillerman.

"Sorry, Dirk. I must come across as a horrible East Coast snob. My experience with the South has been limited to *The Beverly Hillbillies, Hee Haw,* and *The Dukes of Hazzard.* I'm learning, though."

"It's all right, darlin'. My ideas about you Yankees were about the same. Kennedys, Harvard, and rude, pushy folks." He stepped into her personal space, put one hand on her shoulder, and wrapped the second one around her chin, tilting her face up to his. "Maybe we both have something to learn."

"Maybe we do," she agreed, praying her voice held steady. "I'll teach you if you teach me."

She rested her hands on his forearms, the thick hairs under her palms. Need might have flared in his gaze when she touched him, but then it vanished. His lips twitched under his goatee, but he said nothing.

If she didn't back away now, she might never have the strength. She stepped away from him and moved to the desk. Digging in the top drawer, she found what she was seeking.

Sifting through the photos that were still in the package from the store, she selected one and handed it to the giant man still standing by the bookshelves. "There. Not beautiful. I was over two hundred pounds."

The extra weight distorted the lines of her face. It made her more matronly, a woman ten years older than the one in front of him. She had it on good authority that nobody liked a fatty. She was still above average at size twelve, but that was the best she could do.

"Nope. Still gorgeous. Give me more."

Startled, she studied him but saw nothing besides earnest truth in those green eyes. She passed him the set of photos.

His hands stilled when he took out a different group of pictures underneath the first set. This was the Connor Ally, the unguarded woman with a playful, open face. The woman who no longer existed.

Lake Tahoe. It had been the first, and last, vacation she took with Connor. The juxtaposition of lake and mountain was beautiful, but she shuddered when she was reminded of that holiday. That woman, and her idiocy, were gone. They belonged in the dustbin of her history, just like her folly over the man who made them vanish.

Recreation, not relationships.

She was standing with Conner, who had short, sandy-blond hair about Dirk's color. Dirk would never don the pale pink polo shirt Connor had on. Nor did she think he would wear the Dockers and deck sandals. The Ray-Bans and expensive haircut marked Connor as "from money," which she had known when she met him. She just hadn't comprehended what the cost of that would be.

Dirk turned the picture to her. "Old boyfriend?"

"Wow, yeah. That shows how long it took me to finish that roll. That's him. We were in Lake Tahoe."

She bit her lip, worrying the skin under her teeth. Watching him examine the photo, she wondered at the complex series of emotions playing across his face. Was he disgusted that she had gotten involved with someone so out of shape? Someone who had more resources than common sense? Who wore his elite Boston Brahmin roots like a badge?

"Your hair was real pretty. It's pretty now too." His words were quick, as though he was trying to correct a faux pas.

She let it go. "Thanks. Back in the day I was famous for two things. My hair was the second one." She flushed, past compliments surging through her memory.

His mouth twitched, the goatee shifting. "I can understand why your...hair...would be impressive."

Was she flirting with him? Was he flirting back? It had been so long since she'd tried to be alluring she was way out of practice. She was a giddy teenager, making googly eyes at the gorgeous man who filled her spare bedroom.

It couldn't last. Dirk shook his head like a dog and handed the pack of pictures back to Ally. He clapped his hands together and returned his attention to the furniture. "What's with the bookcases?" He pointed to the handmade creations dotting the room.

She followed his finger, and her good mood fled. *Why do you try and do things yourself? We pay people for that. You are ridiculous.*

She fought to keep her voice neutral and was pretty sure she managed it. Butterflies gathered in her stomach, but she pushed them down. "I needed more room, and I didn't have anyone to help me with them. I figured I could make them just as easily. It didn't take too long. I needed the distraction. They were inexpensive—and they match."

His raised eyebrow stiffened her back. She would not tell him the rest of it. No way, no how. That the bookshelves had been a good escape from her tragic memories of Connor was something only she knew.

Paige might suspect, but Ally had never admitted it.

"I'm sure you've got friends with pickups. Doesn't Craig have one?"

"He wasn't in town, so, no." She wouldn't say the rest. She would not admit that she'd never asked Craig to help. She'd needed something to do, and building the shelves fit the bill.

She became aware her voice had risen. The glare she gave Dirk must have told him her hackles were up because he took his cap off his head, smoothed his hair back, and returned it to his scalp.

"It's good to be handy."

Chapter Seven

The air was crisp with a hint of moisture in the clear sky. The occasional thin cloud drifted across the sky. Green and yellow parrots with a red stripe on their bodies swooped in and out of the trees. The cacophony of their cries filled the air.

At Ally's invitation, Dirk had stayed for the day. He shouldn't. He had no business being so easy in her company.

Keep your friends close and your enemies closer. If she put herself in his path, then he would take the companionship, even if she had an agenda.

Dirk and Ally were sitting in her green patio chairs in front of the lanai, the sun's rays slanting across their faces. A light wind blew across them, just an intermittent gentle swoop of breeze ruffling the leaves on her trees. Even though the last rain had been a week ago, the earth of her yard was still soft and damp, moss edging the bricks.

"Why'd you leave Connecticut?"

To his surprise she didn't answer right away. When he gazed toward where she was sitting, her hands were tight on the arms of the chairs. She stared into the distance, staying silent.

Her reaction was outsized for such a simple question. He lifted an eyebrow and waited.

"I didn't have many choices after I finished school.

I wasn't a Yale graduate. My degree was good old Boston University, and that didn't get me very far in the city. I didn't have any desire to go to New York. Los Angeles was..." She stumbled over the words. "Far enough."

He went still, the pain in her simple statements echoing the emotions in her eyes. "There's a story there, or I'm a monkey's uncle. You want to tell me? You don't have to."

She was quiet for so long he thought she wasn't going to speak, then she began in a neutral tone devoid of emotion.

"Sure, I guess. It's not like I keep it a secret. I just don't discuss it without being prompted."

That was a load of horseshit, but he stayed silent. She sure as heck kept it to herself, hidden behind her readiness to be of assistance. Curiosity beat within him, stronger than he liked. The Alanna he was presented with was contained, always doing what needed to be done. This history burned inside her like hot coals. He itched with the need to comfort her. Dirk forced himself to stay where he was.

"Marta—my sister—is two years younger than me. Neither of us was swimming in friends, but we had them. I was on the quiet side, bookish, and she was shy. She would shrink back when someone talked to her. The fact that we had odd clothes didn't help. Mom liked to dress us in discount clothes from Walmart. I was in fifth grade, and she was in third when somehow a rumor got passed around that our mom was gay. The kids started hassling us. Did you guys have that song 'homo we will go, lez-be on our way' where you grew up?"

Dirk shook his head. " 'Fraid that particular ditty didn't make it to Georgia."

"They used to sing that to us in the hallway. Then they decided it would be fun to push us around a little. First one, then another, and then a pack of them were using Marta and me as punching bags." She shuddered. "One day I was walking to class, and this kid Jake, one of the worst bullies, came at me." Her voice was so low it was almost as though she was speaking to herself. "Next thing I'm aware of, I'm being shoved, then kicked through the boy's room door. When a teacher took us to the principal's office, he asked what I had done to provoke it. He did nothing to stop the kids picking on us. He hated my mom for coming to PTA meetings and saying they were all a bunch of fascists.

"It spiraled from there. I tried to ignore it. I had little choice. None of the authorities helped. One class a kid spat in my hair the entire time, and the teacher claimed to witness nothing. Kids threw rocks at us, and the teachers didn't stop it. I learned a long time ago that the one person I can rely on is myself." Her hands stilled, and her gaze was distant.

Dirk gathered his breath to speak, to be stopped by her raised hand.

"There's more."

He nodded, swallowing but saying nothing. The pain on her face was breathtaking. He wasn't sure how he had earned the right to hear this story. He should stop her. When it came time to go, or worse, she wouldn't appreciate him understanding her vulnerability. Yet he didn't move.

Ally pointed to the series of scars across her eye. "Have you ever noticed these?"

He nodded but didn't speak.

"One day Marta and I were going home by one of our secret paths, thinking we were safe. Six boys cut us off as we walked across a bare lot that had iced over. We had nowhere to go. One of them shoved me. I went down, hitting my head on the ice. Then they started kicking us, and I blacked out. We both ended up in the hospital. They had hit Marta so hard that she broke her leg." Her voice grew very soft. "It's not usually visible, but when she gets tired or stressed, she limps. They said I could have lost my eye if I'd struck the ice differently. The impact split the skin in four places and almost shattered the orbital bone.

"That's when Daddy got involved. Mom had kept the bullying from him, but she couldn't hide this. I never understood why she didn't tell him earlier. Maybe she was afraid he'd take us from her or something. In those days you didn't prosecute little boys for assault, but Daddy found out who they were. He went door to door, promising that if their sons ever laid a hand on his daughters again, they would have him to contend with. Their parents claimed they were normal kid fights—and that we instigated—but he scared them. We weren't going to win in court, but they knew damned well if they didn't stop their kids, he would find a way to make it right. My dad is six feet two and built like a linebacker. We moved in with him for two years, to let things cool off. Eventually we went back to Glastonbury where it got somewhat better but not enough. We never meshed with most of the kids, even the ones who hadn't abused us. I didn't go to my prom. I had friends I might have gone with, but it wouldn't have been smart. Some of the worst bullies were the popular kids. Who knows what would have happened?"

"Those monsters should have been prosecuted."

She snorted, a terrible pain crossing her face. "Sometimes the good guys don't win."

"Damn it," he swore. "Damn it," he said again. He'd never felt more helpless than he had hearing the searing story of a brutalized child. His body ached with the urge to do something. Anything. Act. Caught in the grip of a futile rage, he couldn't stay still. He levered himself up and went to the middle of the yard.

"I wish that somebody had stopped those kids. I would have if I had been there. What they did to you."

"That would have been nice, Dirk. I wish I never understood the meaning of cruelty, but I do. It's over, and neither one of us can change it. Thank you for caring, though."

He bowed his head, folding his arms across his chest. He could picture a smaller version of this woman lying helpless on the ice, at the mercy of a herd of boys. He would have been fifteen, already at his full height, and he could have done something. He would have stopped it if he'd been there. A shudder went through him at the idea that this woman could have died at ten, and he never would have had the chance to meet her.

This was not what he expected.

****

Ally couldn't have said why she told Dirk the story. She hadn't meant to, but when he asked, it poured out of her like salt from a shaker. She saved it for those she trusted, who had been in her life for a long time. Very few outside of her circle of friends were aware. Her persona did not allow for tragic backstories.

She could not say why she shattered that image to this man who held her fate in his hands.

You wanted him to know.

It hadn't gone well before. Connor's words still lingered in her mind. *Are you done indulging in the past?* She had been foolish to tell Dirk, but she couldn't take it back now. She'd revealed her tragic past. She waited for him to scoff or mock her.

"I'm sorry. I didn't mean to spoil the morning." She bit her lip, wishing she could rewind the last few minutes. Vulnerability was a bad thing. She had no business giving him a weapon to use against her.

The old jeans he'd changed into last night were weathered almost white in spots. They clung to his form, outlining the curve of his taut rear and the sculpted muscles of his sturdy thighs. He'd left his boots off, and his large feet were bare. He wasn't fat at all, despite how big he was. She wondered what it would be like to put her hands on his butt through the cloth, smoothing it down, and touching those strong muscles.

He took a deep breath, and something twisted across his face. "You weren't the one who spoiled it. My daddy used to tell me that women are wonderful, magnificent creatures, even if us men don't understand them worth a damn. He said that I was a man, and my job was to protect them—make sure they don't come to any harm. If I caught anyone else doing them wrong, I had to stop it.'"

"I doubt you could have. You would have just been on their hit list too, then. Let's talk about something else. I'm sorry I brought it up."

He crossed back under the lanai and stood, his big

shadow falling over her. Then he sprawled in the chair again before turning to face her. "I'm not sorry. Appreciate the trust, Alanna. I get the impression you don't tell this story to strangers."

"I don't. I can't." She reached for something to say that would be neutral. Discomfort danced within her, and anxiety crawled up her spine. "Thanks for listening. Don't let me stop you if you've got plans. I didn't mean to take up your whole Sunday."

She watched the pinpoints of light from the sun dance across his face. The breeze rippled his hair, blowing strands against his neck. The bottom of his shirt hung loose and showed a line of hair on his belly where the clothing separated. A line that disappeared into his jeans. It wouldn't take much to lean over, kiss that skin, and trace it with her tongue.

Stop. It. Ally.

He met her gaze before turning his attention back to the rampaging parrots. "I can stay a bit longer, and then I need to get back. I've got some things to go over for the campaigns I'm working on. Got some ideas I have to get out of my head and into my tablet."

"Okay." She was perversely disappointed, her heart beginning to hammer at the prospect of him spending the whole day with her. "Say the word when it's time to go. What about you? Do you and your ex-wife have any kids?" Realizing how the question must have sounded, she flushed. "Sorry, that was prying and none of my business. You don't have to answer."

"No need for apologies. You told me your deep dark secrets, and it's only fair I give you some of mine. As it happens, no." He started to adjust the cap, then let his hand drop. "I was ready to start a family, but

Belinda wasn't. She was twenty when we got married, still young for that kind of decision. Then we just sort of stopped talking about it. Especially the last two years. Not much talk about the big life decisions. Not much talk, period." He was quiet, his attention on something deep in her yard. "My brother Greg has three. Hellions, all of them."

A visible shaft of pain went through him. The ache was never very far from the surface. It made her want to hold him and never let him go.

"I bet you'd be a good dad. Except for that whole hat thing."

He grunted, and his goatee twitched. She let out a breath, startled at the shaft of relief that went through her at his amused groan. She was lying to him, spying on him at the orders of her boss, yet one more person who didn't trust him.

"Thanks," he said. "I'm grateful."

Gratitude. That was a nice emotion. Nice. Boring. It didn't rank up there with passion, or love, but those weren't emotions that men had for her. She'd learned that time and time again. "You're welcome. Let me as you a question. Why did you come here? This is not a natural fit."

He chuckled, but the sound had no humor in it. "You're right about that. Not like I had a lot of choice, though. I could come to California or join the unemployment line. The other option was my folks, but I didn't fancy working for my daddy. The farm barely can sustain them, never mind a third." He waved a hand vaguely toward her. "Does that answer your question?"

It didn't, not by half, but she had already asked too much. Believing him would make things harder. Rival instincts warred inside her. "Sure."

Something moved behind his eyes, a fire that she would have believed was desire if she didn't recognize all the ways men didn't fancy her.

"What is it that makes you tick? I'm used to East Coast preppie. Like Connor. That's familiar to me. You are not. I haven't figured you out yet."

"Connor. That's the guy in the photos, if I'm not mistaken. The one with the Ray-Bans and a heck of a fashion sense. Was your last guy a bad dude?"

Too late she understood how much her words said. Connor taught her that she was never going to be "the one." She might find a man to marry someday, but she wasn't going to be anyone's idea of their True Great Love.

"He wasn't a bad guy—just bad for me. Connor was my last boyfriend. Talk about a mismatch." These were tricky waters as well. She had to find the right balance of emotions not to seem pathetic. It might already be too late for that. "He was East Coast preppy, with a Harvard MBA to match. We dated for—hmm—about six months." *Five months, two weeks, and six days. Until he dumped you with a text message. It had always been casual, he said—for him, anyway.* "That was a while ago. It's not important."

"Gotcha. I get why he's a bad fit, but your friend at the football party is a good guy. How come you and Craig never dated?"

"He was married when we met. Even if I could have poached, I never would. Then she left, but I was dating Connor. Then I wasn't, but he had a girlfriend. By the time he was free, we had shifted to the friend zone and never looked back."

She tried for a careful, yet friendly grin. She was already weary of the lies and subterfuge but couldn't see a way out. If she was wrong, if her attraction to Dirk was coloring her perceptions and something happened, then she would be to blame. If he was innocent…well, the worst that would happen would be he found out she was a spy with an agenda. Dirk made no secret of the fact that Los Angeles was not his permanent home. Even if they had met under better circumstances, they were a mismatch. As big a mismatch as her and Connor, in a different way.

"Everyone should have friends. It's been a commodity as rare as hen's teeth in these times. Thank you. I just need to be for a minute, then I'll skedaddle." His emerald eyes flashed with a smoky emotion. "You mind?"

She couldn't have spoken if her life depended on it. Swallowing hard, she shook her head.

Dirk leaned back. Ally did the same, stretching out in the chair next to him. She wanted to put his hand on her breast in a silent plea to touch her. In return, she would caress the broad expanse of his powerful chest, testing the strength of his muscles. She desired him so badly she was surprised she wasn't trembling.

After several minutes he opened his eyes and gave her a quick nod. "Thanks. It's a rare woman who understands the power of silence."

She gazed beyond him, her attention fixed on the palm tree, and returned the gesture.

This was not going the way she expected. None of it. This episode of her life was going to end in disaster, and she would be caught in the middle.

She needed to call the rescue group and get herself

a couple of fosters. She resolved to contact them in the morning. Needy cats and kittens were almost always looking for fosters. She'd devote her attention to animals instead of humans. If she were helping needy strays that might otherwise be condemned to an unpleasant end at the shelter, she might not be so inclined to rescue people.

Even knowing that, she couldn't wait to see what the future held.

Chapter Eight

"Hey, Paige," Ally said. "Is he in there?"

Paige acknowledged Ally with a wave, continuing to enter data into her computer. "He's there, but Gordon's with him. I think they're arguing with the distribution company about the number of units they can release. Or something about discounts. It's above my pay grade. You know them; they close the door when money or politics is involved. Give it a minute. I'll message him you're here."

Ally watched as Paige contacted Dirk. "Ally is outside."

Paige's computer dinged. "Dirk says wait for a few minutes. They're almost done." She leaned forward. "What's going on with you and the cowboy? I haven't had a chance to ask you—we don't hang out as much now that football season is over. The whole office is speculating about the exact 'nature of your relationship.' "

This was one person who could be trusted with the truth. Looking around first to make sure nobody was in earshot, Ally spoke in a low, hushed tone. "I am attracted to him, but it's a nonstarter. He's here because he has to be, and I'm just doing my job. It's hopeless. I like him as a person, so it's not terrible. He's a great guy to have in my life. Tell all the gossips that we're friends. Nothing more. Damn it." The last sentence was said for Paige alone to hear.

Paige studied her old friend. "You do you. Just be careful."

She would have said more, but Dirk's door opened, and he stepped into the frame. Both women started.

Dirk's size still surprised her. When he was out of her sight, she made him two or three inches shorter and then was brought up by his sheer bulk when she was in his presence again.

Light from the office surrounded his body in a halo effect, like some huge ancient god holding court in his temple. He filled the doorframe, his head almost grazing the top of it. Her breath caught, and her pulse sped up.

She needed to manage this. She couldn't keep living in a state of longing for a man she could never have. She should find a man who desired her. There had to be some.

The problem was the idea of kissing anyone except Dirk had no appeal to her.

"C'mon in," he said. "Good timing. We just wrestled the distributors to the mat, and Gordon and I were going to start talking about campaigns." He nodded to their boss, who was standing by the whiteboard.

Dirk motioned Ally in. Gordon met her gaze as she entered, his glare telling her she wasn't off the hook by any stretch of the imagination. Nothing had changed.

She gave him a fractional nod as she went by, and Gordon patted her shoulder as she slipped past. They both waited as Dirk tapped his whiteboard.

"Jessica should go for a different sort of campaign," Dirk said to Gordon and Ally.

"Like what?" She leaned against the wall by his bulletin board. Tension manifested itself in the rising of her shoulders, and she made a conscious effort to shove them back down.

Sun caught at the edges of his hat, glinting off the rounded shapes that made up his hatband, sending prisms of light scattering across the walls.

"The gal is a size, what, nothing, right? What about clothes? Get a 'Susan the Magician' baby T-shirt out there in one of those yellow colors. Jess can model it. I think she'd be good in yellow. Her blonde hair and brown-eyed combination should get her a fair amount of attention."

Jealousy flooded Ally, rendering her incapable of speech. Dirk had noted how attractive Jess was. Of course. Ally wondered if Jessica and Dirk would make a good couple or a bizarre one. Would Jess link herself to someone with his reputation? Ally considered what Jess thought when Dirk was in the room. She might be attracted to him. To the best of Ally's knowledge, Jess didn't have a boyfriend.

She hated Jessica Baker.

I think she'd be good in yellow.

She cleared her throat, striving for a normal tone. "I like it. We can work on that for her signings." Her voice was sharper than it should be. She fought from screaming at the idea of the two together.

Gordon shook his head. "We don't have much of a travel budget, so it would be local stops or video calls."

"Won't be much good here," Dirk said after studying Ally. "We should get her out somewhere where her brand of sassy country is going to be appreciated. First things first. Alanna, you work on getting interest in her so that signings would make sense."

She nodded.

He clapped his hands together. "Good. Ready? Break."

Gordon looked at Dirk, then at Ally when she laughed.

"You don't watch football, do you?" At the negative shake of his head, she continued. "That's what they do in the huddle at the line of scrimmage." He appeared even more confused. "Never mind, Gordon. It's a sports thing."

Gordon left, and she detached herself from the wall to follow, but Dirk's voice stopped her.

"What's wrong?"

"Nothing." She was aware that her voice still had a sharp edge.

"Sure, and I'm the Easter Bunny. What's wrong?"

"Nothing," she said again, trying to summon her reserve of smiles. She found one that was close to what she was trying to portray, if a bit too bright. "I just didn't understand you were interested in Jess. It might make it complicated."

"Do you mean…me and Jess? I'm not. She's a sweet thing, but she's too young for me."

Her sigh of relief was audible. She fought to keep her emotions from showing.

"Oh, here." He reached into his desk drawer. "I got you something."

She held the box in her hand, goose bumps playing over her body. The hairs on the back of her arm rose as the flesh did. It had been a long time since someone gave her a present without expecting effusive thanks in return. She was reminded once again that this man, for all his rough-hewn mannerisms, had an innate sensitivity that she'd not often experienced.

"Thanks," she said before she opened it. "That's very considerate of you."

Canting her hip, she half sat, half leaned on his desk. A pink pig figurine, no longer than an inch, rested on her palm. It had folded ears, a curly tail, and sad eyes. The pink was vibrant, with a glossy glaze that made the color stand out even more. Underneath the pig was a card that read *Hagen-Renaker* with numbers below the words.

She was unable to control a trembling of her lips. "Thanks. This is great." She hoped the sheen of unshed tears didn't show.

"I got to admit I didn't find it at a thrift store, but I hope you'll overlook that. You got nothing in the office pig related. Figured this could go on your computer. Keep you company when I'm not around. His name is Wilbur."

"That's the perfect place for him." She managed to get the shaking in her body under control and directed a nod at him. "Plus, the perfect name. You're an amazing man, Dirk."

She opened her mouth to say more when the building shifted.

****

The room swayed in a rocking, dipping motion. The vertical blinds on his window clacked together in staccato patterns, moving at random by the unexpected shaking. His whiteboard vibrated. The motion reminded Dirk of the rolling of a ship deck, except they were in his office and not out at sea. The sensation was like being hit with vertigo. The room was off balance with no way to right it, the corners of the room tumbling and swaying.

"What the hell?" He gripped his desk, his knuckles going white on the hard oak.

Alanna was still, staring out the window. She had set the pig down, and her hands were tensed on the edge of his workstation. Her shoulders had pulled back by her spine, but she was still leaning on the desk in the casual posture she'd adopted a minute ago. Her head was angled in a listening posture.

The moving stopped after a few seconds, but the blinds still moved in slowing arcs, coming back to rest over the next minute. Ally still had her head tilted to one side, lips pressed together, breathing rapid.

"Earthquake." She focused on him. "Small one, under four points. I bet the fault line that runs close by here is where it originated. Otherwise, we wouldn't have felt it at all. The sounds the big ones make are scary."

"Sounds? Fault line?" He was aware that his voice had gone up an octave but was helpless to stop it. Panic beat inside him on bird's wings. The ground was not supposed to move.

"Sure. With the big ones you can sometimes hear them coming before they arrive. It's a roaring sound deep in the earth, like an underground freight train. It's real unnerving."

He was sure she could tell by the shivering of his body that this one had been scary enough.

"California is laced with fault lines. Can't escape them. From what I can tell, one goes straight under my house."

He started to say something before shaking his head, words failing him.

Her lips quirked. "Dirk Roberts. Don't tell me you're scared of a bitty little quake like this one?"

Her summation should have reassured him, but it didn't. He took a deep breath, trying to deny it. The fact was that his heart was in his throat. The sudden sway of an earth always meant to be solid under his feet scaring the crap out of him. He stared at her, fear sweat trickling down his face.

Their co-workers called out Richter numbers—their guesses for the strength of the quake. Someone turned their TV on, and he heard through the open door that the quake was so small the newscasters hadn't even broken away from the daytime soap operas to report on it.

He was stunned by the matter-of-factness of it all. To them, this was nothing more than an ordinary occurrence, a minor nuisance to be shaken off—forgotten.

One more reason to get the hell out of Dodge as soon as possible. Earthquakes. *Ain't no cause to be in a place with crap like that.* His plan had been to stay just long enough to establish his reputation again and then return to the place he'd called home for almost fifteen years.

He didn't know if he was going to make it.

"I'm sorry," Ally said. "Earthquakes are scary. The first one I went through was tinier than this one, and my heart pounded for a solid hour. My boss at the time believed I was shaking her desk. After a while, though, you get a sense of them. I'm not saying you ever are comfortable with them, but you learn to tell what you're in for. You figure out how to tell if the rolling motion is a tiny quake here, like today's was, or a big one somewhere else." She leaned over until her face was close to his ear. "Those big temblors are the ones that stop your heart. Luckily, they don't happen very often."

Her breath was warm over his cheek, and he resisted the urge to turn his head to kiss her. She surprised him by being so calm about it. With the panic still flaring across the inside of his chest, he couldn't imagine it, but it must come about.

She gripped his shoulders and shook him. He forced himself not to lean toward her.

"Are you okay?"

He nodded, the sides of his mouth pulling down and then going flat again.

She moved away from him. Taking up her spot on the side of his desk once more, she picked up the pig figurine, absentmindedly running her fingers over the smooth contours. "Better?"

His heart was still pounding. "Yeah, thanks." If his baritone was rough, he could attribute that to the quake and not the faint waft of perfume that lingered in his nostrils. Not to the sudden, swift hardening of his body when her hands caressed him.

"All right, so if we're back on solid—not so solid—ground, we should get back to what we were doing." Her attention was on the figurine and not him.

He wanted to slide his fingers through hers. Human contact was what he needed. He could not, would not, get it from Alanna. His voice was gruff, the drawl thick. "We're good. I got the net up," he continued, gesturing to his computer and tugging his keyboard toward him. "Let's take a gander at the upcoming release slate for the studios for any movie soundtracks we can target."

As they surfed the net, Ally glanced over at his TV.

A video was on. The woman framed in the TV was beautiful, with piercing blue eyes and a fringed short haircut that suited her face. She was dancing in front of a fiery house and belting out her tune with all her might.

"Wow," she murmured. When Dirk's brow furrowed, she spoke again. "That woman is so gorgeous. I'd love to be her for a day to see what it's like to have every head turn when you walk in the room."

"She's nice too. Belinda was a big fan. Marlon arranged for us to meet her at an awards show. I never got to work with her, but I hear she's easy as these things go." He turned his attention to her while his browser loaded a web page. "She's no more gorgeous than you."

She snickered, waving a hand toward him in dismissal. "Dirk, please. That Southern charm is great, but don't be absurd. There's chivalry, and then there's ridiculous."

He chuckled. "Okay, yeah, she's gorgeous. But you're real."

She rolled her eyes in a gesture he was coming to know well. It almost hid the flash of pain that went through her eyes. Another man might not notice it.

"Yeah, right. Like any guy would ever choose me over a goddess like her."

He paused, his hand on the mouse, his body going still. He fought to control the words that went through him. Ones he should not speak under any circumstances. "Alanna. You have everything a man is after. Don't ever think otherwise."

"Of course, I do, sport. Why, I can't even listen to all the answering-machine messages of men pleading to take me out. They're beating down my door. It's a veritable conga line out there." She held up her hand when he started to speak again. "Thanks for the pep talk, Dirk, but please, no more."

He drew a deep breath and swiveled in his chair to face her. She backed up a step when he rose. His hands flexed as he fought against doing what every hormone was screaming for him to do. *Kiss her. Touch those red lips and find out for yourself if that is lipstick or her natural color. Taste her mouth. Do it.*

"I'll let you in on a little secret, Miss Alanna Wilson. I like you better at a size twelve than at a size six. A man doesn't feel like he's going to break you. You were stunning in those pictures but not because of your weight. Because of this." He gestured to his own lips, fighting to keep from touching her. "That smile was out of this world."

"I smile," she protested, offering one that didn't work. The twisting of her lips fell short of being called anything but ghoulish.

He leaned down until he was face-to-face with her. The brim of his hat grazed her forehead. Sun broke over them and dappled the edges of her shoulders with its rays. *Don't do it, man. Don't do it.* "Yeah, you do." He touched her lips with one callused finger. "Here." Then he tapped the skin next to her eyes. "Not here."

He wanted to haul her into his arms and kiss her with everything he had in him. That was madness. "Am I wrong?"

"No, Dirk." Her admission was low and must have

cost her a great deal. "You're not." She shook her head when he started to speak. "But…" She trailed off, tears turning her eyes shiny. Before he could say anything, she spoke again. "Let it go."

He grunted and rose. No doubt she'd already told him more than she intended to. He shouldn't push her. They only had one direction to go, and that was a one-way ticket into disaster. He backed away and moved to the door. "You do what you need to. If you change your mind, I'll listen."

"Thanks, Dirk, I appreciate that. More than you understand."

He grunted, the need surging in him like a tidal wave. A vulnerable Alanna was twice as gorgeous as the efficient one who bustled about solving problems. If she gave up her secrets to him…all of them…he had no idea how he could resist her.

"Then that's all that need be said."

She exhaled, and he detected relief mixed with a different emotion, one he couldn't quantify. He hated to think what it could be.

"What are you up to tonight?"

"I've got a date with a TV dinner and an efficiency apartment," he managed, the idea of that cold, sterile place appalling. "Then I think I'll go for a run. You?"

"Pretty much the same, minus the apartment. Spin class for me, then a delicious store-bought salad. Then off to bed."

Bed. That sounded better. Hers. With her naked and open to him. Where he could explore her until neither one of them knew up from down.

This madness had to stop.

Chapter Nine

She drummed her fingers, fighting the urge to call Terri. Ally couldn't talk to Paige, not when Dirk was her boss. Craig didn't trust Dirk and couldn't be objective.

She hadn't physically spoken to Terri in a couple of months. They'd texted and hadn't fallen out of touch, but those were more surface conversations. This would be a leap.

Without allowing herself to think of the foolishness of her actions, Ally called Terri. It rang once...twice...and then went to VM. She didn't leave a message. She'd send a text to Terri later.

When the phone rang with Terri's number, Ally almost didn't answer it. She could pretend she missed the call and then "forget" to call back.

"Hi there, stranger." She took a deep breath, trying to summon a false front of cheer. Now that she was speaking to her old friend, she wondered what she should say.

"Hi yourself. You called. I had to stir something continuously for one minute and couldn't break away to answer."

"You and your recipes."

"Yep!" Terri had a lilt to her voice. "It should be delicious when it's finished. Too bad you're not closer. I could give you some."

"I'm in Sherman Oaks, not Mars. You're not too far away."

Terri chuckled, and that lilt was still there. "You know how we who live in West Hollywood are about going 'over the hill.' " Her mock shudder was loud enough to be heard through the connection. "It's just not done."

"I didn't recognize when I bought a house in the Valley that I was dooming myself to exile in the middle of the desert."

"Your choice." Terri's tone suggested that she was teasing. They had been good friends for a while. The drift was as much due to Ally as anything else. She didn't think Terri knew about Connor, and she would keep it that way. At least for now. Their history went back further than that, and Ally's terrible taste in men was legendary.

She shared that in common with Terri.

"True. It's closer to work. I don't regret it."

The Valley, Ally? That's where you live? Why am I not surprised?

She needed to shake Connor's disapproving voice. He was gone and had been out of her life for two years. He shouldn't have power over her anymore.

"You shouldn't. Buying real estate in Los Angeles is everyone's dream. You were smart. What's up?"

She hadn't fooled her oldest friend after all.

She took a deep breath, about to detour the conversation into work topics before mentally shaking herself. She had come this far, and she might as well go all the way.

"What do you know about Southerners?"

Terri's whistle of surprise pierced through the

speaker. "That's not what I was expecting."

"What do you mean?"

"Everyone is aware you should have gotten that job. You were robbed, and if I'm the first one to tell you, then that's ridiculous. I thought you were calling to ask what you should do."

Ally sorted through her emotions before speaking. "You're right about that. I do feel cheated. You're a VP—how did you do it?"

"I got lucky. I've got an honorable boss, and I work in a tiny company. It's part of the reason I left the big players. Kai can't pay what the majors do, but he makes up for it with titles and great references. You have it rougher. Your corporate ladder is steeper. The Southerner you mention is the new VP, right? Dirk Roberts, if I'm not mistaken? He's the one who took your job? Are you asking for advice on how to handle him—besides kicking him to the curb and taking what's yours?"

She could steer the conversation to the workplace and never have the deep discussion. She almost did so. "It's more complicated than that."

The silence went on too long, and Ally was about to fill it with words before Terri whistled again.

"Oh wow. Got it. Nothing like a guy to screw things up. What can you tell me about Dirk?"

Ally sorted through her impressions, from his height to his manners to the way she tried to dislike him and couldn't. It all wrapped up into one neat bundle. A delectable, edible package. Ally was grateful Terri couldn't see her blush. His tight jeans didn't hide his manhood, and from all indications he had a fine penis on him.

She. Would. Not. Say. Any. Of. This. To. Terri.

"He's Southern. He wears a Stetson and says ma'am and y'all a lot. He's got good manners and is super polite, but that could be a front. Gordon has me watching the guy in case he messes up."

Terri let out a breath. "You're his watchdog? That's not your role. You've got enough to do without adding babysitter to your job description. You should say something to Gordon. That's not right."

"I earned that promotion. Gordon never said I would get it, but I believed I would until he hired Dirk. At first, I thought I'd find out about him, and then he would be gone." She paused. She couldn't tell Terri she liked Dirk. That would be way too embarrassing.

"You like him. I hear it in everything you're not saying."

"No, I..." She stopped herself from saying the falsehood. "I guess I do. I didn't expect to, but, Terri, you'd have to meet him. He's so tall and broad, like a football player. He's got this great ponytail that reminds me a little of when I was dating Harris, except Harris didn't fill out T-shirts so well."

That provoked a snicker from Terri. Ally relaxed. She hadn't even recognized her shoulders were hunched until her friend chuckled at her not-very-funny joke.

"I don't think I've met anyone from the South. Not deep south like you describe. You're dating him, then?"

Ally shook her head, even though Terri couldn't see it. "Nothing like that. We are co-workers, and even if we weren't, he wouldn't be interested in me. We're, well, I guess we're friends, except I'm spying on him. He might be a bad dude—the usual complicated stuff that always goes along with my relationships."

"We never do make it easy on ourselves. You're smart not to date him if you're co-workers. That would be an HR nightmare."

Terri's phone beeped. Relief coursed through Ally. She'd already said too much. She shouldn't be dumping all this on Terri. Her friend had a point. "You should take that. Let's get together soon."

"Sure. Maybe a hike? I need to get more exercise."

"That sounds great. Later."

Ally didn't know whether she meant the last words or not but found she was smiling when she hung up.

When her phone rang again with Dirk's number, she considered her options. Whatever else was going to happen, she'd figure it out. She could let it go to voice mail, or... She answered on the second ring. "Hi there. What are you up to?"

"I was thinkin' of getting out of here for a spell. What are you doing today?"

Later, Ally watched Dirk's pickup approach, the heavy hum of a powerful engine cutting through the air before the late-model vehicle cruised to a stop in front of her house. Her porch was set back from the road, giving her an opportunity to observe him. Shielded by the shadows, she sat in the rocking chair in the back corner of the porch, watching him come toward her.

He was wearing a white tank top, ball cap, and jeans, those long legs ending in sneakers. The outline of the muscles of his torso were visible under the thin cloth. Light from the mid-morning sun streamed across his face as he started up her driveway, glinting off the sunglasses on his face and burnishing his naked shoulders with brown highlights.

Ally admired him as he ambled toward her with that rolling, panther's walk. It reminded her again how sensual he was. He always moved as if to music, the sway of his hips matching a tribal beat.

He was halfway up before he became aware of her presence on the porch. Coming to a halt, he found her sitting in the shadows and grinned. She flushed. Then she waved to him. He touched his cap toward her and continued up the driveway.

"I didn't expect you to answer my call. Glad you did. I was sick of my own company." He removed his sunglasses at the same time, then fitted them over his cap.

"No worries. I was talking to a friend but just doing house stuff. I was thinking we could go for a ride. There's some beautiful scenery when you get out of the city. It's not the Blue Ridge Mountains, but they don't suck."

The teasing words covered her desire to run her hands over the expanse of his chest to feel the short hairs under her palms, the textures of his male nipples. Then replace her hands with her mouth, tasting his broad, powerful form, seeing if he liked being licked as much as she did.

The twittering of sparrows competed with the brisk wind that rustled through the branches of the trees. That same breeze lifted the edges of his ponytail, sending individual strands dancing.

"Those are some gorgeous mountains. We used to go camping once a year. My family, that is. My brother still goes. He's teaching his kid, my nephew—Jacob, that's his name—to fish. There's a sweet fly-fishing spot not too far from the campsite. Those were good times."

"You told me, but I forgot. How many children does he have?" She tried to conceal her thirst for knowledge about Dirk by ducking into the shadows and busying herself with gathering her dirty dishes. She wished she had a hat to hide behind. That would be useful.

"Three. Jacob is my godson as well as the oldest. He's going on twelve now."

"How old is Greg?"

"A bit under forty. They got married young, but they've been together since high school. They were each other's first loves. Good stuff, that."

The words filled her with a strange melancholy. Ally's first love, if she could call it that, had been an unsuitable bass player. Her next had been Connor, and that hadn't ended well. Her track record with men sucked. She was in danger of adding to that statistic if she kept going. "That's nice. It restores my faith in humanity. Let's go. Ready for a trip, big guy?"

"I sure am. I can't wait to see these mountains. From here they're brown blobs."

"You are such a Southerner."

He was too near and way too tempting. She pulled away before she could do something she would regret. Or…not regret but set herself up for heartache.

"C'mon, I'll open up the sunroof, and we'll get on the road."

The 170 gave way to the 5 North, and they were headed into the outlying regions of Los Angeles. The day was clear and bright, the sun streaming in through the sunroof warming their skin. Dirk sprawled in her passenger seat, his ponytail dancing with the wind.

The sun heated the top of her head and gave her a sense of peace. "Those blobs are getting closer mile by mile. That's them ahead of us." She waved a hand toward the vista. "The city does end when you get to them." Wind drove leaves across the freeway as the tires counted out the miles. His longing for the land was evident on his face as he watched the open vistas.

The music emitting from her speakers was a country singer named Tracy Byrd.

"Darlin', I am going to get you some Hank Senior and Johnny Cash. Introduce you to classic stuff."

She flashed him a grin. "That would be great. You like Tracy, don't you? You can change it if you don't." She gestured to the device, unwilling to admit to him that she'd loaded it up on the genre to try to impress him. She shouldn't have bothered. He knew more about the genre in his little finger than she ever would. He had the advantage of almost thirty-five years of indoctrination.

The song was called "Watermelon Crawl."

"He's good. There's a line dance to this one. I'll teach you if you're willing."

A negative shake of her head was her answer. "Me, the Queen of Grace and Beauty? Line dance? Nobody wants to witness that, Dirk."

She'd used the old quip hundreds of times. It usually made her audience laugh. She waited for him to join in, but instead he frowned, a muscle jumping in his jaw as he clenched his teeth.

"Sure," she amended. "That would be fun. Thanks."

"Alanna, I don't get what all you've been told about yourself in the past, but you shouldn't listen to any of that cow pucky. Don't let anyone ever take you down to their level. You do what makes you happy, and the rest will come. Let's go back to that honky-tonk, and I'll show you. You willin'?"

She nodded, unable to speak. The stone lodged in her gut shifted, sliding away. "Sure. I think I've done the Electric Slide a time or two. That I can do. Is this one like that?"

He chuckled, and fire flashed in his eyes before they were once again shaded by the cap. "It's a little harder, but you'll get it." He peered at the mountains, which were growing closer with every mile. "I think I can make out a tree or two on the hills. I can't wait to see what California mountains look like."

****

He didn't belong here in this land of goddamn sunshine. Earthquakes were the norm, and the city went on forever. He needed to be home. If not in Nashville, if that city was still barred to him, then in Georgia where the hot days meant tea on the veranda and a quiet afternoon on the porch swing.

Not this...metropolis. Not where there were millions of people—and none of them were real.

Damn it, but he needed friends. He liked his own company well enough, but the last year had been a nightmare.

Alanna should not be one of those. He should be turning down her offers of lunch, coffee...goddamn cartoons on a Friday night. Awareness of the woman in her sweats and bare feet continued to seep into his consciousness when he was least aware of it.

Like now.

This wasn't how his detour to California was

supposed to go down. He intended to endure it for a year, doing what was required to restore his reputation and then get the hell out of Dodge. Now a curvy, delectable blonde had him imagining things he had no business wondering about. Claiming, bodies, and hot nights rolling around between the sheets. Of fisting his hands in her hair and tugging her to him. Of tongues and breasts and…

He groaned, trying not to look at the woman as he lengthened against his jeans. He hadn't been with a woman since before he left Tennessee. He'd gone out on a few dates after his divorce, but his heart hadn't been in it.

Damn it. He was here for a reason, and it wasn't the woman. He should stay away from her.

Dirk couldn't remember the last time he'd experienced this kind of attraction to a woman. He'd been married for the better part of the last decade and had still loved his wife when she left him. That sort of thing didn't easily fade, but it had been killed in the divorce. After several months of no attraction to the opposite sex, he expected that maybe that the sexual side of him had died along with his reputation.

Now he came face-to-face with Alanna. The attraction roared through him, growing every day.

Damn it.

To his astonishment, snow was on the ground when they got into the mountain. Ally parked by the side of the road and got out of the car. She went to the view and rested her arms on the guardrail that stopped her from tumbling into the forest just beyond. The snow wasn't so thick that it hung from the branches of the pines, but the layer was just enough to delight his senses.

"If I'd had any idea I was going to be in the mountains, I would have gotten a pass for the year. I'm not sure what we can or can't do, but it's legal to park here. At least there aren't any signs."

"Y'all have to pay to enjoy the forest?"

He couldn't tell if the gaze she turned on him was empathy or frustration. She'd been real good about dealing with his snipes about California to this point, but maybe he should take it down a notch. She liked it here, and for her sake, he could try a little harder to be charitable. California wasn't to blame for the pickle he was in.

"Don't you? I mean, park passes, camping permits, all that? Or do they not do that in Georgia?"

He nodded. "They do. Right you are. Let's go down into the snow."

She followed him down, and when he took her elbow to help her over a fallen log, she gave him a stare that made him stop breathing. The look was as smoldering as a firepit, and his gut clenched. He shifted, letting her go. He picked up a stick that had fallen from a nearby tree.

He shouldn't get involved with Alanna—even if she was going through what he was. That wasn't a sure thing. She might be friendly, but she was like that with everyone. He wondered if anyone else noticed the core of reserve at the heart of her.

Or he was imagining it.

He wasn't staying, and her home was here. She was a Yankee, and he was a down-home Southern boy. She liked this crazy place with its heat in winter and its year-round sunshine. She wasn't about barbecue, country music, and Stetsons. She was about the Red Sox, Boston Tea Party, and all things Yankee.

He had no reason to get involved, except one.

He might never act on it—and a wise man would not—but he couldn't deny the truth. She was a warm breath of sunshine in his cold world, and he desired nothing more than to yank her into his arms and kiss her until her eyes unfocused. Plus, so much more.

She bent and picked up a handful of snow. The way her butt showed in her jeans when she crouched almost made him groan aloud. She had a man's wet dream of an ass—rounded with luscious curves. Baby got back, as the old song went.

Then she flung the snow at him with a mischievous grin and took off.

"It's going to be like that, is it?" He grinned, grabbing some himself. The snow was cold in his hand, trickling into the calluses that had begun to fade due to lack of outdoor activity. He would have to do something about that. He'd slacked off on the gym as well. Being out in the cool air made him understand how much he'd been wallowing.

No more. Starting tomorrow he was turning over a new leaf. He might not have chosen to be in California, but he was here, and he should make the best of it.

He hurled the snow at Ally, and she giggled. Desire surged within him, pounding through him on a wave. He almost groaned, bending down to grab more snow to cover the tightening of his body.

When he glanced up, a hastily packed snowball was heading his way, striking his jeans jacket. His breath puffed out in a dash of white from the cold. He grinned when the thing thumped his shoulder and broke apart on contact. She gave him a smug grin. The delight on her face sent all his nerve endings racing. He hadn't realized until then that she was helpful to everyone but was never easy around company. This was the first time he'd seen Alanna let loose.

Something had happened to her to make her this way. It had to be related to that Ray-Ban-wearing, smug guy in the pink polo shirt. He already hated him.

Then he had no time to think as the pine tree sent a shower of needles down on her. They tangled in her hair and slid off her body. He expected her to complain, but all she did was laugh again. Their time up here in the mountains had changed her into someone carefree, an echo of the woman she must have once been. He longed to learn that side of her.

She shivered, rubbing her arms with her hands.

"You're getting soaked," he said, wishing they could stay out here for the rest of the day.

Or the rest of his life.

"Nonsense. You're just trying to avoid getting pelted again."

Then she flung another snowball at him and took off, picking through the ground as she ran. He caught up to her, swinging her around. She stumbled and fell into him.

If he had been on fire before, now a full-on conflagration rushed through him. His body surged at the sensation of her curves. Her breath rushed out, warm and cold at the same time. Her lips were so close. He needed only to shift forward minutely to be kissing her. He peered into her eyes. Awareness flared in them as well. She smelled of snow—and woman. In her gaze was the promise of home and family. All the things he hadn't expected to find in Los Angeles.

He wanted to kiss her. He had to kiss her. Just as he was closing the distance, she made a low sound and backed away. He released her, trying to be glad that it hadn't happened. It would commit him to something he wasn't prepared for. He couldn't see what good could come out of being with her, yet he craved it like fire.

"I guess I am getting cold."

He sighed, trying to control his reaction. The time was lost. He should be grateful he hadn't done something stupid.

He longed for the missed opportunity.

"Can't have you catching your death. Let's get back in that car of yours and put on the heat. Then you can take me farther up into these mountains. Unless you need chains?"

She shook her head.

He should be grateful they hadn't breached the gap. Once they did, there would be no going back.

He told himself that's what he was feeling. Gratitude.

Sure, he was.

Chapter Ten

She managed to put the near kiss out of her mind. Maybe that flaming interlude had been fiction. Even if it hadn't been, the notion was a bad idea no matter what. They were co-workers, she was watching him, and she was after his job.

"Promo guys are hustling for adds in all the key cities for Jess' release," Dirk was saying to Gordon. "Best to target satellite radio, although we'll try for local, of course. They might play her as an up-and-coming new artist."

"She's getting a bunch of hits on her site. Social media is going well. She's got a good presence with the fans. We need to keep on the fan club. We need their votes. The upcoming conference dovetails well."

"Sounds good," Gordon said.

Ally had Jess' social media pages fired up, requesting Jess at all their radio stations, writing her in on the request lines, putting her at the top of any online polls they could, and hustling for any corner they could. Some of it might have been unimportant to a bigger label, but every little bit counted.

"Hey I'm starving," Ally said. "Why don't we break for lunch? Or I could order in."

Dirk shook his head. "Can't, too much to do before she comes out Tuesday. We've got our list of stations we're targeting. What do you think?" He pointed to the whiteboard behind her.

The places they targeted were in the South Atlantic and South-Central states. Good, solid country places like Georgia, Kentucky, Arkansas, Virginia. Texas, Oklahoma, Mississippi. Cities like Atlanta, Savannah, Dallas, Roanoke. Not New York, Boston, or Los Angeles where country was not popular.

"Looks good." She let her shoulder graze his arm, gazing up at the man standing next to her. She hoped her attraction didn't show but doubted that. It must be blindingly obvious to anyone in their vicinity. She had to stop this. That near kiss... Had he desired it as much as she had?

Giddy, dizzying sensations swept through her, and she fought to keep her expression neutral. "I'll have Jess stay on top of the fan club. I think we're ready for the conference next week. Travel to Austin is all set, and I have hotel confirmations for Jess and the band. No news about awards shows, but that's a long shot anyway."

"It's not needed, but it sure would be nice. There's time. Keep working on it. We've started tracking the charts," Dirk said.

"Hey, Ally," Gordon said. "Are you doing something different with your hair?"

Dirk glanced at her, then at the mass of honey blonde. Her hair now waved over the back of her neck, at least an inch past what it had been when he first met her.

She was growing it. She told herself the change was for any number of reasons, but that was nonsense. She did it because Dirk liked long hair.

This had to stop. She should not be trying to please

a man. She knew firsthand how badly that went.

Don't try to punch out of your class, darling. You don't have the pedigree. The words of one of Connor's Ivy League friends echoed within her. The woman had been there on a business trip and made it clear that Connor's little middle-class girlfriend was annoying. She shouldn't have been surprised that they wound up together. It had been inevitable.

"I got bored with the short hair," she said, running her fingers through the lengthening strands. "Someone reminded me that I was pretty with long hair, so I thought I'd try it again." Avoiding Dirk's attention, she focused on the whiteboard. "What's going on with the promo ad?"

"Promo ad is good. I'll get the final version next week. We got seven thousand 'Susan' shirts ready to go to the hotel for goodie bags. I got ones for you and Jess. Will you wear it at the convention?"

"If you will wear one too," she said. The image of him in a lemon-yellow T-shirt with a picture of a woman holding a wand saying *Susan the Magician* on it brought a smile to her face. She suppressed a chuckle at Dirk's mock black glare from under his hat.

"Doesn't go with the Stetson." His drawl held the rounded tones that meant he was amused.

Ally turned to Gordon after flashing Dirk a mischievous grin. "I think Dirk wears too many primary colors, don't you, Prez? A lemon-yellow T-shirt might jazz up his image, get him in touch with his feminine side. Doesn't that Western store on Van Nuys Blvd. sell all sorts of colored Stetsons? We could get one to match."

"I'll give you feminine side," he growled.

Dirk couldn't control the twitching of his lips, a tic that told her he was enjoying being teased as much as she was relishing teasing him.

Gordon's gaze darted between them. "You get Dirk into a yellow T-shirt, and I'll make sure you get a bonus."

She turned her attention to Dirk, tilting her neck up in a pleading pose.

He chuckled, shaking his head slowly. "Sorry, darlin', not even begging would get me in one of those frilly, flippy colors."

With a sigh, she relented. "Let's get back to it. I've got a lot to do before the convention." She should be happy for her win. The fact that she was going to the conference and not Dirk was a good thing. All she had to do was keep at it, and she would get what she was owed.

Even if it came at his expense.

"Too bad about the T-shirt. Catch you later." She ducked out before Dirk could make a smart retort.

****

"Hey there, stranger!"

Ally lifted her hand to wave at her friend. Terri August strode toward her, flashing a smile as she did so.

Even at this early hour on a Saturday, Runyon Canyon, in the hills above Hollywood, was peppered with hikers. Fog had rolled in during the night but was beginning to burn off as Terri arrived, sending wisps of white air arcing with the wind.

"Hello back," Ally said in return. She realized how long it had been since she last saw her friend. IM and text didn't count. They didn't take the place of face-to-

115

face interaction. She'd let Dirk and her job consume her, far more than she should.

Ally and Terri were dressed in sweats and loose-fitting T-shirts, their curls tied back with scrunchies.

"Ready to work off some angst?" Ally said after a very brief hug. She hadn't had much physical contact with another human being in a while.

"Oh yeah," Terri said.

They headed through the large iron gate with burglar bars at the top of Fuller Avenue that signaled the start of Runyon Canyon on the Hollywood side. The path was wide, tan dirt packed solid by the feet of many pedestrians in this popular area. A few hikers, some with dogs, surged around them. Most of them ignored the two women strolling on the trail.

Their slower speed meant dogs bounded past them, and fitness-minded joggers did likewise. As they walked, the sun rising, the city started to reveal itself behind them. The sight never failed to inspire Ally. Los Angeles Basin was spread out below them, the view going on for miles on a smog-free day. Today the basin lay shrouded in mist and shadow as the sun broke over the horizon, revealing the vista below.

They had opted for the easier trail, but even the so-called less-strenuous path was still a workout to Ally's unused muscles. She wasn't out of shape, but she had let exercise slide like she'd let many things go.

A dog scampered up to her. She reached down to scratch under the dog's ears and stroke its head. The dog rolled on the ground, its jaw open.

"Sooooo…" Ally said, the word drawn out until she got Terri's attention. Rising, Ally smacked her hands to rid them of the dirt. She started walking again,

116

with Terri following. The elevation and workout combined made them pant for breath.

"Sew buttons?" Terri grinned at the old joke.

"How's Clarke?" Ally cast Terri a sidelong glance.

Terri was quiet, and Ally wondered if she'd overstepped. When Terri accepted her invitation, Ally hoped it would restart their friendship. Maybe she'd waited too long.

"He's fine," her friend said.

"Don't go all gushy on me, Terri August."

"Hah. It's hard to explain. We're figuring it out. What about you?" Terri ran her hand over a bush.

Scrub and trees were around the trail, and bits of dirt were kicked up by hikers.

Ally bobbed her head. "Same shit, different guy."

They continued to walk, the ground rising under their feet, taking them higher into the Santa Monica Mountains. Graffiti dotted the landscape, reminding Ally that the underbelly of the human race was still out there.

"Yes, about that." A teasing smile played across Terri's face. "How's the label? Is the new foray into country music going okay? How's, er, Dirk?"

Ally's steps slowed before she picked up the pace. She shot Terri a cheery grin that she didn't feel.

"The label is great. They're—we're—getting there. I think we might make it." She paused. "Sorry you guys aren't doing that well. I hope Apposite recovers. As for Dirk, he's a guy. The only thing we have in common is pro football." She said the last one with a wry twist of her lips.

"I bet there's more to it. He sounds unlike Clarke as I can imagine. I'm having trouble visualizing the friend I knew ten years ago with the woman who would have a crush on a Southerner. You were a rocker chick."

"Not anymore."

The rise continued upward. The San Fernando Valley could now be seen in front of them. The greenery of the vista was beautiful, even with a thin layer of brown covering the valley floor. The sun was peeking out to their right, making its way up the sky. Ally and Terri walked in silence for a minute.

Barking behind them made both women jump. Terri let out a whoop of laughter, startling Ally. She took off running, sprinting for the top of the mountain before them. A dog chased her, its tongue lolling, before lagging behind. Blood tingled in her veins, making her body sing. Sun warmed her right side, sweat flashing on her arm. Her legs ached, but she ignored that and relished the burn. It meant she was active. She ran past the low scrub and tough grasses dotting the approach to the top. Then, with one final burst of speed, she reached the highest point. She stopped, her heart pounding and her breath coming in short bursts. The unfamiliar exercise caught up with her, and she almost buckled, her legs threatening not to support her anymore. She bent over, sucking in large gulps of cool air, the sweat starting to diminish.

She made her way to where Terri was standing. She laughed, a surprised, delighted sound, at the glee on Terri's face. She hadn't seen her friend so open since before the Clarke fiasco.

"My God, the view, Ally," Terri said, so loudly that more than one person turned. "It's beautiful."

"Yeah. I've got to go out of town for a few days,

but we'll get together again when I get back?" Ally tried to keep the hopeful tone out of her voice. Their friendship had limped along on IM and texts, surviving but not moving forward for years.

"I'd like that." Terri rose. She clapped a hand on Ally's shoulder and just as quickly withdrew her palm. "I'd like that a lot."

"Me too."

Terri held out her arms. Ally embraced her awkwardly, two friends out of the practice of touching.

"Thank you," Terri said.

"You're welcome."

Peace washed over Ally. She could do this. She could reach out and have neglected friends respond. Maybe the sting of what Connor did could be put where it belonged—in the past.

****

The conversation with Gordon played in Dirk's mind like a mantra. One he didn't care for.

"I had to let her go to the conference," Gordon had said, stopping Dirk on his way out the door. "I've got to give her something."

Dirk paused, leaning against the doorframe and summoning his neutral exterior. He was well aware that the movement made him appear forbidding—and he didn't mind. If his goatee made his downward-slanted mouth seem that much more disapproving, he was okay with that. "I'm not sure I take your meaning, partner."

"Ally. I thought about sending you to the convention, but I didn't think that was a good move. She's still sore about losing out on the promotion, and I wanted to throw her a bone."

"I shouldn't be going anywhere as a representative

of your company right now. Our company," Dirk amended, heat rising at Gordon's casual dismissal of Alanna's contributions. "She works her tail off for this company. You should give her more than a conference where she has to haul ass to keep up. I've been to those conferences. They're a hell of a lot of work."

Gordon shifted in his ergonomic chair, an expensive model that must have cost the company more than a few pennies. Behind him the large-paned windows looked into what was euphemistically called "downtown Burbank" where hills beckoned several miles away.

A memory of their recent excursion to the mountains surged through Dirk. He'd wanted nothing more than to kiss those lips made even redder by the cold. They'd matched her charming red nose. The package of Alanna in the snow had been hell to resist.

He cleared his throat, shifting as longing caught him off-guard, sending heat washing through him.

"She's good at that. Ally's a workhorse." Gordon said nothing else, but Dirk wasn't fooled.

"Got that right. I'll say my good nights, Gordon."

Dirk drove the short distance to the efficiency apartment, pondering his next move. He should steer clear of this—he knew that. Whatever Alanna did at the conference, she could hold her own.

He had no business calling in reinforcements.

He put the phone on speaker while he rummaged for something to eat. He could make some mean Georgia barbecue, but this place wasn't set up for slow and low. He'd have to fend for himself.

"I did not expect to see you come up on my caller ID."

Ryder Bingham's smooth tenor made Dirk smile as he pulled out the meager contents of his refrigerator. Sandwiches. It would have to do.

"I did say I would call, hoss."

"Pardon me for saying so, but you're not the touchy-feely type."

He knew something—someone—he'd like to touch. All over.

"I called to see if y'all was going to the conference." Dirk examined his compiled meal. Alanna would have better offerings. He bet she would prepare something better than a few slices of ham and cheese on bread if he called her up.

"Yeah. It's local, so I've got no excuse. I can't tell the label it's too far for me to travel when downtown Austin is almost in my backyard. Why? You coming? Want to meet up at Stubbs or something and get some good old-fashioned Q? Not that Georgia stuff you think is so great."

"I was just hankering for some Georgia barbecue, but I'm out of luck here. Naw. I ain't going. I don't want to be part of any sideshow. I'm still laying low, much as I can in a city with musicians on every corner. I called to see if you'd be of a mind to do me a favor."

The rush of the line was the only sound for longer than Dirk would have anticipated. He was about to retract the question when Ryder spoke.

"If I can." Ryder's tone was cooler than it had been.

"Aw, no need to get squirrely. I'm not asking for me. I was hoping you could keep an eye out for my co-worker—the one you met that day at Roscoe's. She's heading your way, and she's going to be all by her lonesome."

Now the rushing sound was a bit more charged—or perhaps that was Dirk's imagination.

"The pretty blonde with the nice...eyes?"

Dirk's growl came from deep inside him, a primal response that he was unable to control. He bit into the sandwich, visualizing how Ryder's face would change if he advanced on him.

Slow your roll, tiger. You've got no say here.

"Alanna Wilson is her name. Keep your eyes where they belong. In your head and not on my co-worker."

Ryder's chuckle rumbled through the tiny apartment, making Dirk's jaw set. *Damn it.* He'd said too much.

"Ally. That's what she called herself. Sure, hoss. I'll keep an eye out for your...co-worker. She's a nice gal. Any friend of yours, etcetera."

"Thank you kindly. I appreciate it."

When Dirk hung up, he slammed his fist down on the counter. Calling Ryder had been a tactical error, but he couldn't let Alanna walk in there alone. He felt better knowing someone would watch out for her.

He wanted to be the man to do it, but that wasn't in the cards.

Chapter Eleven

The press of bodies in the Austin Convention Center and on the streets surrounding it got on her nerves after a while, but that was the nature of an event this large. She was surprised that Shatter Sound Records had allowed her to go and not Dirk. Chalk up one for company tenure. Generally new artists were in attendance, over a thousand playing throughout Austin. Ally usually took an hour or more to wind across the convention floor as she was stopped every few feet by friends or colleagues saying hi and talking shop. At one point she thought she'd glimpsed Marlon, but if the Earthy Cry executive recognized her, he made no sign.

Jess had finished up her interviews and was in her hotel room, resting for the night. Sunday would be another round, then a late-afternoon plane trip home. Ally and the local retail rep from the label would stay with her to facilitate the interviews. Ally had already visited the BBQ place where Jess' ten-o'clock show was taking place, and made sure that she and the sound guy ran through an abbreviated version of the set. An almost overwhelming array of bands was available for showcases, and Ally needed to make sure Jess got proper attention.

On the plus side, Dirk had called her to tell her about an online Austin article that mentioned buzz-worthy artists, including Jess.

The entertainment possibilities were so varied a person could stay up all day and all night and not take it all in. During the day hundreds of showcases of signed and unsigned bands took place, all trying to get a foothold in the door. Film screenings and a trade show took place in the same time frame. Invitations went out to parties and more parties until the streets around Austin were thick with patrons in various stages of inebriation.

The panel was well attended with about three hundred fans jockeying for position. Ally waited for the panel to end. When it did, Ryder caught her eye and held up his finger for her to wait. Some artists were hustled out by their managers, but Ryder joined the circle of fans waiting for him. A short, dark-haired, intense man glared at Ryder as he made small talk and flirted with the group. Some of them had buttons with Ryder's face proclaiming them to be *Ryder's Raiders*.

Ryder motioned her over when he was done and gestured to the man standing next to him. "Have you met my manager, Mike Richardson?"

"Ryder, we should get going," he said in a clipped tone.

Ryder turned to look at him, then back at Ally. "I'm going to hang with my friend here for a while, Mike."

Mike scowled but said nothing.

Anxiety pounded through her. She twisted her hands together before speaking. "I hope both of you will come to Jess' show tonight. I'll be the one running around like a madwoman, losing ten years of my life hoping the showcase goes well."

"I'm going to go check on Warren if you don't

need me."

At Ryder's nod, his manager left.

Ryder watched him go and then turned to her. "I was going to call you or turn up at Jess' show tonight."

"That would be great. I'll introduce you guys. Hey, I thought I saw Marlon—is he here?"

"He's here. Let me guess, he pretended not to see you, right?" He laughed when she just gave the singer a tight nod. "Marlon and I have a civilized disagreement about Dirk. He thinks I'm a fool, and I think he's an ass."

She couldn't help a tiny chuckle. "I'll agree with the second statement."

"Me too. I don't have to like him; I just have to work with him. That's how the saying goes. I liked working with Dirk better. He doing okay?"

She made a noncommittal gesture. "He's settled in. Los Angeles is not his cup of tea, but he's getting by."

His narrowed gaze took in her hesitant response before he gave a brief nod. "It's like that, is it? I wondered. The two of you lit up Roscoe's."

She ducked her head. "It's like nothing. We're co-workers." She lifted her gaze back to the singer. "The company would frown on that, and I have my eye on a promotion."

He waggled his eyebrows at her. "Mm hmm. Over fifty percent of new relationships start at work. You could do a lot worse than Dirk. And he you."

"You seem pretty sure of that."

"Few things in life are certainties, but this one is a solid bet." Ryder studied her. "The promotion is that important to you?"

The idea of achieving her goal slid further from her

mind every day, but she didn't let that show. "I earned it, and more."

Ryder signed an autograph for someone hovering and then endured a selfie before returning to the conversation.

"Sometimes when we get what we're after, we find it's not what we expected. I checked out your campaigns after I met you. You're good. You're wasted at Shatter Sound. You deserve better." He shook himself as though dislodging a stone. "Who am I to talk? I don't know shit about managing my life. Listen, you hungry? I need to eat."

Something moved behind his eyes, a sorrow so profound she almost reached out a hand to him. Then his bright smile was back. She would have been fooled if she wasn't familiar with the method as well.

"Sure. I'm starved. We need to go to sound check, then I've got time."

After they got some takeout barbecue, Ryder gestured to a spot beyond them.

"I've got something to show you if you're not squeamish." The sun was starting to set over the tall buildings of downtown Austin. His hair was pulled back, and his Austin City Limits ball cap was low over his face. An eagle-eyed Ryder Raider wouldn't be fooled, but the casual passersby didn't note the platinum artist.

"Me?" Ally laughed out loud. "You're talking to the original tomboy. Climb up buildings? Sure. Walk beams across swamps? Sure. Let a scorpion crawl across your arm? Sure. Although that one took a little doing."

"Good." They walked with a crowd heading in the

same direction.

"This is quite a sight." They were near the river. All attention was focused on the underside of a bridge called the Congress Avenue Bridge. The expanse was large, with crevices underneath it.

The sun continued its downward spiral. Ally heard faint sounds.

Then the sun set behind the buildings, and thousands of bats exploded out of every crevice, wheeling down out of the bridge before soaring skyward to join their brethren. She watched in stunned silence as the bats poured out of the bridge, calling to each other before settling into their ancient rhythm. There were so many that they darkened the sky.

"Oh, wow…" she said as the last of the bats joined their kin down river. "Thanks, Ryder. That was amazing."

"I figured you'd like it. Not all women would, so I appreciate you. There's over a million bats. They're Mexican free-tailed bats, and they just came back from Mexico. It's quite the tourist attraction."

"Well." She glanced at the bag she still held. "Why don't we find a comfortable place on the riverbank and eat this delicious smelling barbecue? You can tell me more about the bats—and about Ryder."

They ate in silence at their spot near the bridge, wiping gooey barbecue sauce off their hands every few bites, until Ally summoned the courage to ask Ryder the question that had been on her mind for so long. "What was Dirk's ex like?"

He toyed with his food before responding. "I met her a couple of times at Earthy Cry functions. She struck me as a soft-spoken Southern woman, with a backbone of pure steel. Steel magnolia." He took a bite of his beans before continuing. "They were happy. At least when I first met them. The last two years they were married, something was different. Dirk would never talk about it, but something had changed. When I'm in love, I'm always aware of where my partner is. At the end of their relationship, Belinda didn't care where Dirk was."

She went quiet, glancing over the now-empty bridge. The crowd was dispersing, packing up their lawn chairs and their bat signs and heading back to their cars. The river grew quieter with each passing minute. The sun was setting lower in the sky, darkening the air around them.

"That's a shame. I don't get it. My parents didn't work out, but true love is out there. That's why I gave him a chance. Dirk, that is." Ally paused for a minute, the flippant words striking a discordant note she didn't like. "I felt like I knew Dirk right from the beginning. He was familiar to me somehow. Have you ever experienced that?"

Ryder's intake of breath was harsh. His pupils had dilated to pinpoints. "Once. Just once. Ally, you find that, you hold on to it. You hold on to it, and you don't let it go. Trust me. I wish I had."

"What about you? How come you believed him when Marlon and ninety-nine percent of Nashville didn't?"

His words were measured when he replied. "Marlon is an old-fashioned good old boy with strict moral values. The idea that a boy he took under his wing could betray him like that didn't sit well with him. My understanding is he tried to make it out like maybe

Dirk hit her or some horseshit like that. Dirk is huge and can appear really dangerous. He didn't get anywhere with it, because Belinda didn't back the lie. She did that much for him anyway." He opened his mouth before shaking his head. Whatever he'd been about to say vanished. "My daddy hit. I recognize the type, and it's not in Dirk. You ever been around an abused dog?"

She nodded. "Sure. I do rescue." She took a deep breath. "I've been abused myself." She gestured to the scars on her eye. "By all rights I should have lost my eye, and my sister should have been crippled." Telling Ryder the story, she was amazed at how little power it had over her anymore.

She was gratified by the sympathy on his face.

"When I grew up in Snook, we were dirt poor and lived in a trailer. A family lived in a trailer not too far from ours, and they got a puppy long about the time I was seventeen. They screamed at him and struck him all the time. I watched that dog go from a romping, playful little thing to a cowering cur." His lips turned down. "You weren't in Nashville. I was. Every time Dirk got figuratively kicked, his jaw would harden that much more, and he would retreat that much further. That's not a man who did what they say he did. Often the bigger the crime, the more bluster a man had. Dirk was a man kicked, not a man guilty."

"I see."

"Oh, that dog. That old tick hound's name is Blue. He's probably lolling in the doghouse right now. He's older now and spends a lot of time sleeping. Right around the time I moved to Austin, the dog disappeared from the trailer."

Her squeal of delight was unfeigned. "I would be proud to call you friend, Ryder Bingham."

"You are my friend." He reached for her hand. "When Dirk and I would go play pool, he would talk about things like love, honor, and tradition. Dirk and I, we're both romantics at heart, believing in soul mates and destiny."

She paused before continuing. "I read a story once about a guy who was trying to locate a device that would show him the face of his soul mate. When he does find it, he learns who she is all right. Spoiler alert—is it okay if I go on?"

He nodded, an amused grin playing over his face.

"She lived a hundred years prior and died long before he was born. I have no illusions about my future, Ryder." He started to speak, and she shook her head. "That's just how things go sometimes. It's like you said earlier. You've got someone in your past—I can sense it."

He said nothing before letting out a low breath. "Thing about Blue was when I first took him, he hid in the corner of the apartment. Every day he would come closer to the bed, expecting to be hit but wanting affection so badly too. That the blows never came took a long time for him to understand. Man is just an animal. Give Dirk time."

"What about you?"

"We're not talking about me. It's not important. Hang in there. Let your Blue learn to trust the warmth of your fire."

She was shaking her head even as he spoke. "The problem is that my last boyfriend taught me to believe that what a man says is what you go by, even if his body is saying something different. He couldn't get enough of me, but I wasn't good enough to take out in public or admit our relationship anywhere but behind closed doors. He told me so on more than one occasion. I believed I could change his mind. It's no spoiler alert to tell you that I was wrong. At least with Connor we had similar backgrounds. With Dirk we have nothing in common. Dirk hates Los Angeles. I have no experience with the South. He isn't staying. My future is there."

"Is it?" he chided. "That's for you to decide. We need to get back. Duty calls."

"Sure." She rose, and he came with her.

"I regret letting the woman that I love go every day. Just think about it, okay? I'm a romantic, and you've got that same quality. You deserve to be happy. Take a chance."

She busied herself with a wet wipe, avoiding his gaze. "I should go get Jess and head for the club." She was evading the question inherent in his comments but was unable to form a coherent sentence.

"Shucks," he said, a wry grin on his face. "I'm not trying to scare you off. Consider the subject dropped. I'll go with you to visit Jess. Ain't got nothing to do after these last interviews."

All during the showcase, when she wasn't busy running around, she thought through what Ryder said about telling Dirk the truth. Always, every time she considered it, she flashed back to Connor. *I never said I loved you, Ally. How could a guy like me ever love a girl like you?*

Dirk wasn't Connor and wasn't the kids who tormented her, but the net effect was the same. She couldn't take the chance. She'd stick with what she had.

131

To risk more meant risking it all. She didn't have the courage.

Chapter Twelve

He shouldn't miss her this much.

He and Alanna had no future. She was a damned Yankee from Connecticut. She didn't know about the country or Georgia barbecue or his family's way of life. She lived in, and by all accounts loved, this godforsaken place he'd found himself.

He had no business thinking about her.

He wrote on his whiteboard and then erased it. Wrote it again. Erased it again. Jess would be better served at a bigger label who had the wherewithal to properly handle a country artist. This joint had no clue what to do with her. Gordon vetoed most of Dirk's ideas, and he wasn't sure why Gordon had brought him on.

Maybe to get eyeballs on this place. All publicity was good publicity. It wouldn't be the first time Dirk had been used.

He wrote more notions and left them on the board. Alanna should evaluate them and give her opinion.

He set the marker down and went through his paperwork. Answered some emails. Tried not to pick up the tablet and surf for any online articles from the conference. He'd already seen one he didn't like—his pal Ryder and a woman laughing together at some crazy bridge where bats flew out of.

Alanna and Ryder were an unlikely combination,

but Ry always did like the smart ones. It wouldn't be impossible. The women Ryder had been with that lasted more than a week were often from the industry. Ryder never told Dirk about his past, and Dirk never asked. They didn't have that kind of relationship. Matter of fact, he didn't have that with anyone. 'Cept Alanna, and that was an impossible daydream.

Dirk wanted to shatter the tablet into pieces on his desk but tossed it down before he could go back to the bookmarked article.

He focused on the whiteboard. They needed more funds; there were none to be had. Jess was not going to do well if Dirk didn't get creative. Well, that's what he was there for. He started writing again, anything that crossed his mind, ignoring the almost impossible desire to call Alanna just to hear her voice. He had to stop this.

He couldn't imagine doing that.

"Those are some zany concepts."

Dirk nodded at the new entrant as Gordon crossed his arms, a puzzled expression on his face.

"Just noodlin'. Sometimes it makes the creative juices flow."

Gordon stayed silent, and Dirk set the marker down, turning to study his boss.

"Something on your mind? Our update meeting isn't until tomorrow."

His boss opened his mouth and then appeared to change direction. Whatever he really wanted to say vanished as he tapped the whiteboard. Dirk thought about asking but dismissed it. He wasn't a man who rocked the boat without cause. Getting in and out of Los Angeles was still the goal.

Wasn't it?

"I was wondering what you're going to do next. We've got to wrap Jess up and move off her onto the next artist." He handed Dirk a folder. "These guys are what I am excited about. A five-piece band with two lead singers. They're country the same way the modern guys are, in that they're more rock than country. There's good crossover potential there. These guys are real winners. They have a little controversy, so I thought you'd be good to work with them. Since you're familiar with that."

A muscle jumped in Dirk's jaw. He'd taken many blows through the last year and always told himself he was just biding his time.

That time stretched like eons in front of him. He longed to be done with his sentence in this place. If he was being honest, he had to admit that California wasn't so bad—present company excepted. He'd been there three months and had to do at least nine more to make this stick.

He wasn't sure he was going to make it. If not for Alanna, he might have been gone already.

Alanna, who might be flirting up a storm—or more—with Ryder Bingham. He had great affection for his friend but hated him at that moment.

"Sure, you're the boss. The launch is imminent, and then I can start on this. She's doing her showcase tonight at the convention, and Alanna is keeping an eye on her. I thought we were throwing more resources behind Jess, but that ain't my hill to die on. Still, I'm curious. Are we backing away from Jess? Why did you send Alanna to the conference if you're going to dump Jess?"

Dirk didn't like the way Gordon's attention shifted.

He hadn't known Alanna when he took the gig. He hadn't understood who he would hurt. Now he just had to ride it out and hand the job back to her when he left.

He feared leaving Alanna was going to be one of the hardest things he had to do.

"We're not discarding Jess, not yet, but it's got to change fast, or we will. As for Ally, she's fine but limited. I'm sure you know what I mean. She gets mired in the details or thinks way too far outside the box. She doesn't get the big picture, and her ideas are crazy when she goes creative. She's perfect for stuff like ushering talent to conventions and doing the paperwork. She can focus on the small stuff. We needed a bigger mind to make the artists pop. There's a reason we brought you on."

Dirk was silent again. He'd learned a long time ago that, at his height and build, saying nothing was intimidating.

Gordon flushed, stumbling over his next words. "Don't get me wrong. She's great, but it's just…well…she's…"

Female?

"She does a good job. This company would be lost without her." Dirk's flat tone dared Gordon to contradict him.

Gordon did not. "We've given her raises and promotions through the years. She started as an assistant ages ago. That limits her. She came up through the ranks, and there's only so far she can go."

Goddamn it. Dirk resisted the urge to tell Gordon what he really thought. *More flies with sugar, Roberts.* "She's worked hard. She deserves to go to the next level."

Gordon chuckled. "Then you'd be out of a job. I need Ally right where she is. She does the best doing what she's doing. Let's talk about these ideas. There are some that might be salvageable."

After Gordon left, Dirk tapped his phone on. With the time difference from Los Angeles to Austin, she was most likely sleeping. He hoped she was. The alternative was unthinkable.

Maybe he shouldn't phone, but he could send a text. That way if she was snoozing or occupied, she had the option not to answer.

Nah. He wanted to hear her voice. Before he could change his mind, Dirk pressed her number.

To his relief, she responded right away. He grinned at her reply, trying to ignore the rush it gave him.

"Just finished up. Your pal Ryder jumped on stage with Jess for the last song. It's already in the news. Great for Jess—and the label. What are you up to?"

He needed to ask more about "his pal Ryder" but would not. Could not. The answer might leave him broken.

Of all the things Dirk had imagined might happen when he went to Los Angeles, having a thing for one of the natives was low on the list.

She wasn't a native. She was worse. She was a Yankee.

"Just getting ready to head out for the night. Got some new ideas for Jess I want to run past you when you get back. I…value your input." *Even if Gordon doesn't.*

"Thanks. I'd love to hear them. Are you behaving while I'm gone? No roping steer or chasing horses? Maybe a visit to the Horseshoe Saloon?"

He grinned. "Nope and nope. Although I did see a mounted cop when I was in Hollywood. Made me think about riding."

"There's the Equestrian Center in Burbank. We can do that when I get back."

He should say no. God, he should.

"I'd like that. Bet you're getting an eyeful of the rural life in Texas."

"Nah. I've barely left the area. Hotel, convention center, Sixth Street. The end. Listen, much as I love talking to you, it's getting late, and I've got an early call tomorrow before my flight. I'll phone you when I get back."

"Sure." He let the phone drop and tried not to admit the rush that went through him when she'd said, "Much as I love talking to you."

Man, he was in trouble.

He shouldn't call again. She said she had stuff to do in the morning, and he shouldn't keep bugging her. He'd already disturbed her once. Twice was going to seem desperate. He should let her be.

Even as he struggled against his inclination, he was fighting a losing battle.

When she picked up, the TV was audible on the other end, and he let out a sigh of relief. He hadn't waited too long. "Hi, Dirk. Twice in one day. To what do I owe the honor?"

"I was wonderin'… You're probably too tired. I got no business asking. I was gonna ask if you got any plans when you get back tomorrow, but you're going to be worn out, I'm sure."

The image of Ryder and Alanna kept bouncing around in his head. He wanted to see her as soon as possible and look her in the eyes. He would know the truth if something had happened between her and his old friend. He shouldn't care—but he did.

"I might need a nap, but I get in pretty early. I don't have any food in the house, so I'll need to do something, and I can't imagine going to the grocery store when I get back. I'll want to check in on my new rescue mama cat and kittens and make sure they're okay, but after that, I'm open. You have an idea under that hat of yours?"

"Tell me about that place you used to go to. The rock one. What's it like? Would you be up for going tomorrow?"

"The Whammy Bar? It's a dinner place and a club with music and good food. It's where the leftover rockers go to drink and remember the old times."

"That too much for you? I have a hankering to check out the place."

She should say no. He was imposing. He should retract the suggestion. He had no business getting any more mixed up in her life.

"What time tomorrow?"

Dirk hung up, happier than he could remember being for a long time.

****

"That's some outfit," he said, taking her hand to help her out of his pickup. The lot to the club was lined with cars with the valets bustling about. "I've never seen you in a dress before, and that one is stunning."

Ally had almost called him to cancel. She'd had a thousand reasons ready, but when she saw him in the pickup, they'd melted away. She'd coughed to hide her awareness and made small talk as they drove into

Hollywood. She was glad it was dark out and her flare of need would be hidden by the shadows. She wished she had a hat.

She'd opted for a simple, black, sleeveless dress that had a shirred waistline and a straight skirt that fell two inches above her knees. She didn't know designers, but this dress was more than she usually paid for stuff, so she assumed it was someone with a little bit of renown. Not that it mattered. Dirk wouldn't know what store she bought it in.

He helped her down, then tucked her hand into his elbow. She imagined she felt his breath on her hair, but that had to be an illusion. Her head swam with all the ways she desired this man.

"Thanks," she said, "you're looking good yourself." He'd left his hair down and his head bare. A white long-sleeved shirt matched with dark black trousers and black cowboy boots were his choice of attire for the evening. She wondered if he felt naked without the hat. She wouldn't ask. Never ever.

"I like your hair down."

His grunt was her only answer. She should be used to it.

A surprised doorman met them at the door, welcoming Ally with a bow, before declaring that it had been way too long. He ushered them to a maitre d', who found an open table. She watched Dirk take in the place. The restaurant was dark with black booths along each of two walls and tables bisecting the middle and aisles on either side. The booths were deep, their cushions plush. Modern artwork hung on the walls. A rock song, its beat steady, could be heard over the speakers. Intermingled odors of food and sweat lingered in the air.

Before they could get to the table, she was grabbed from behind and hugged.

"It's been ages," a deep male voice said.

"Hi, Harris." She stepped free of him. "How've you been?"

After a heartbeat she said, "Dirk, this is Harris. Harris, Dirk."

A look of what might have been concern moved over Dirk's face.

Harris was in his mid to late forties, a tall man with long, frizzy, blond hair and a thin face and body. Time had not been kind to him, but his craggy not-quite-handsome features still drew the eye. She eased away from him, putting space between them.

"I'm all right," Harris said, his attention back on her. "You are sexy enough to eat."

She tossed her hair, feeling it settle over her back. "Harris, you old reprobate. You're unstoppable. What's new?"

"Not much. Doing studio work and a solo album. Trying to find true love."

"Sure, you are," she agreed. This was a game she was used to and found an old expression she had perfected back in the day. Terri had called it "playful disbelief." "Right after you get naked with the Budweiser twins."

Dirk snickered, and her attention went back to him.

"Harris is one of the rockers I was telling you about, coming here to swap stories about the good old days of the '80s."

She was flirting with Harris, something she didn't do now. Ally didn't flirt with anyone. To her surprise she fell into it naturally, like muscles that were still there but hadn't been exercised in a while. Dirk's hands clenched at his sides, and she cleared her throat.

"I do have something going on. Clarke, Steve, and I are doing a one-off show," Harris was saying. "I'll put you plus one on the list if you'll come." His quick glance at Dirk was almost comical.

"I wouldn't miss it for the world. Thanks." She wagged her finger at him. "Word is spreading fast, even though it hasn't been announced officially. More important, I'm friends with Terri August. I've got the inside track, you might say."

Harris stared at her, no recognition on his face.

"The woman at the label, Harris. The one dating Clarke."

"Got it," Harris said. "She's different than she was. I almost didn't remember who she was. That's Clarke's cross to bear. Better him than me, even though she's not the same person she was ten years ago."

"None of us are," Ally said.

"You guys thinking of recording?" Dirk asked, focusing the attention of the bass player back on himself. "You did some great stuff."

Harris gave Dirk an appraising glance. The two men locked gazes, and she watched as Dirk let the seconds play out as he often did, using his silence as a weapon.

Harris broke first. "We'd like to, but there hasn't been a lot of interest. Washed-up, old rockers and all that. We were going to get signed on Clarke's label, but it's failing, and Kai said we'd better try elsewhere." Sorrow moved behind his face and then was gone.

"Apposite is going down? Damn. That might be an

interesting catalog to pick up," Dirk mused.

"Hey now. That's my friend you're talking about."

Dirk started, and then his hand went to his head as though he were going to lift his hat. It fell when it came up against nothing. "Sorry." He reached into his back pocket and fished out a business card.

Harris scanned it, and Dirk's full name registered on the man's face. "None taken. She has no power to stop it."

Dirk grunted and focused on Harris. "I got some connections left at some labels. Not the majors, but some of the indies. If it's not too much of a step down, I'd be happy to make some calls."

Harris tapped the card with long fingers. "We're not having much luck. Clarke's rep still lingers."

"Don't worry about that. I'll get you in."

"You're that guy…" Harris said.

Ally stepped into the breach. "Dirk didn't, Harris. Trust me."

"Got it. This industry sucks sometimes." He held out his hand to Dirk, who shook it. "I'd be grateful if you set something up. I'd owe you big, man."

"Not me. Her. I'm doing this for her. You'd owe Alanna." He squeezed her shoulders in a light but possessive caress. "It's time to get us some grub, darlin'. I'm hungry enough to eat my horse."

She didn't correct Harris' assumption that they were dating.

They slid into their booth and picked up their menus. Before she could open hers, he spoke.

"How long were you lovers?" he asked.

Her head came up, and she was aware that shadowed pain tore through her face. She fought for control, smoothing out her features as he watched.

"A year, with a second year of off and on," she said. "I was in love with him, but he was incapable of being faithful. We broke up when I found out that he came here during the week and went home with whoever happened to be around. It's not that he didn't care about me in his way. He said he loved me—and I believe that he did—as much as he was capable of. After the second year he told me that my expectations were too high, and we should end it." Her mouth twitched, and a sigh escaped her. "He was nice about it but made it clear that I wasn't enough for him."

"But..." The word seemed torn from him. "You were flirting with him."

"Maybe I was," she agreed. "Old habits die hard sometimes."

"He hurt you."

"He did, but he can't help being the way he is. Sex comes too easy to these guys, even in this day and age. Harris is a sweet man but a musician, with all that that implies. Was I really flirting?"

"I call this flirting." Dirk imitated her hair flip, and she laughed.

"Guess I was at that," she admitted. "Sorry about that. That's bad form to flirt with a guy when you're...out...with someone else."

"I liked the action but not the dude. I got insight into who you once were, even though it meant you flipped your hair at your former lover."

Her laughter quieted at his words. She couldn't say what lay in his heart, but those sentences suggested...no. She wasn't going there.

"Careful with the hair flip, cowboy, as yours is

longer than mine." At his grunt of laughter, she grinned. "Harris and I are friends now, of a sort, Christmas cards plus occasional phone calls. I don't bear him any resentment. Not like Connor."

Connor. Always Connor. She had to remember him. He'd turned her from a laughing, flirtatious, sexy woman to mile-high defenses and careful words. He'd made her walk away from the playing field, leaving behind her heart and her body.

Not that Dirk wanted those things. No matter what he said.

"You started to tell me about Connor before. Care to tell me the rest?"

Ally met his gaze. She'd have to tell him sometime, and it would be better with a drink.

"Connor was a Harvard MBA, Boston elite, and the son of one of my dad's friends. When he came out here to take a job in entertainment finance, it made sense that I show him around." She shivered, her hands moving back and forth across her biceps.

"I showed him the sights, including my bed. He was so different from the musicians I had dated that I believed he was the one for me. He was nice at first, very attentive and complimentary. Until I fell for him. Then it changed. A lot of that is on me. He said that we were nothing more than a good time, but when we were together—alone, anyway—he couldn't keep his hands off me. Then there were times like when he would flirt with women in front of me. Or when he pushed me off to the side when a pretty lady was around and still expected me to be available at the end of the night for sex. I let him use me. I kept coming back even after his friend, the lady he's with now, told me I didn't have a chance."

"That's harsh." His fingers clenched on the table, but he didn't otherwise react.

"Harsh, but accurate. Turns out he was just as bad as the prior guys but in a three-piece suit instead of spandex. We were lovers for six months before I found out that the woman I mentioned was more than a friend. She was Boston blue blood like him. She said that we could finish our little rendezvous, and she'd be waiting when he had the peasant out of his system. He never understood why I stopped after that. I'd taken everything else, so why not that? It may have taken me too long, but I'd had enough." At Dirk's snort of approval, she tried to keep her voice steady. "I realized then that I sucked at picking men. Here in California, we have a law. Three strikes, you're out, and I was out. To make matters worse I piled on a bunch of weight, men stopped checking me out, and I retired from the game. Ta-da. That's all folks."

The expletive Dirk uttered wasn't audible, but she saw the motion of his lips.

"Connor had better pray he never meets me in a dark alley. In my world," he said, his voice gentling, "where I'm from, they teach you when a horse bucks you, you get right back on."

"Sure. I got back on after Harris. I got back on after the next guy. However, when three different horses throw you, you learn that riding is not good for your health." She snapped open her menu.

"Besides," she said after a brief lull, "it's not like you and I are doing that dance, so why don't you leave me to my pathetic dating life? Let's decide what we're having for dinner. The pizza is amazing." Her words were harsh, with biting stings that were meant to deter further questions.

He focused his gaze on the menu. "Point taken. What else is good here?"

Chapter Thirteen

When dinner was over, Dirk eyed the glass doors that led to the other part of the club.

"C'mon, cowboy, let's get you onto that dance floor calling your name."

He leaped up, eager to burn off some of the sexual energy rolling inside him. He had to let it out on the dance floor rather than do what his every cell was longing to do.

The thump of a heavy beat was apparent before they went through the separator. Inside, he took her hand, tugging her toward the dance floor. They wound up in the middle of the tangle of bodies. Mirrors were on two walls, and an exit door led outside. A deejay was behind glass, headphones on, moving to the beat as he chose songs from his playlist.

The room was warm and damp. A tang of mingled body odor scented the air. He could feel her body heat just inches away. He'd disregarded how close they would be. Maybe he'd chosen not to focus on it. The pulse of awareness—and danger—lurked in his mind.

"Be right back." Dirk moved to the glass panel where the deejay sat, slipped the man some dollar bills, leaned over, and made a request. He returned to Ally and, despite her quizzical head tilt, said nothing.

Standing half a head above the tallest man in the room, he was aware he commanded attention. He moved from side to side with the beat, arms up by his shoulders, hands raised.

Ally began her own low, rolling movements, her center of gravity carrying her down, then up, her hips rocking. He watched in delight as she gave herself over to the music, finding the rhythm and swaying with it.

The next song started with the beginning strains to Grandmaster Flash's "White Lines." A slow smile spread across her face.

When the tune was over, she went to the deejay. After the next song ended, Lynyrd Skynyrd's "Sweet Home Alabama" came on.

Dirk grinned at her, his heart and soul lifting with satisfaction. "You're a brat."

"You know it."

They danced to Guns N' Roses, to Parliament, Bob Seger, Van Halen, and more. At some point, someone bumped into Ally, and she stumbled. Dirk's hands went to her waist, steadying her. He didn't let go.

"Easier this way," he said, his voice a rumble under the music. "Can't have you falling in a heap at my big ole feet."

His heartbeat sped up, and he was breathless, desire coursing through him on a wave. He feared it would be him who stumbled. She put her own hands on his hips. He started moving again. He couldn't make love to her, but he could work it out on the dance floor. His gaze lingered on hers as they moved together in response to the primal beat.

The song ended, and the lights brightened, but Dirk continued to hold her. He couldn't do anything else. They were just dancing. That was innocent enough.

He shook his head, the lie falling flat in his brain

with a thud.

"Jesus, get a room!" someone said next to them.

Her breathing was thready, a frantic pulse visible on her neck. Red patches of color lit her cheeks. Her nipples were tight, standing out under the cloth.

She wanted him.

The emotion was everything he had feared—and hoped.

All the signs were there, including the high color and shallow breathing. The recognition sent a hammer blow through him, tightening his body until he found it difficult to breathe. All the reasons he'd told himself to stay the hell away from her fled like deer from a gunshot. She was so desirable standing there, her hair damp from dancing. Her damned sexy body was just inches away. He doubted she would say no. Not the way she was staring at him. His hands trembled with the force of his need.

He released her from his grasp, and she took a step backward away from him.

As he watched, her face smoothed out. She offered him a bland, amused appearance so sincere he wondered if he hadn't imagined the first. That needy, thirsty woman vanished. Even in the dim light, her half smile was present—one that he'd seen a thousand different times. One that was nothing more than a cover. He considered calling her bluff and stepping into her personal space to kiss her until she begged for more.

"Lord have mercy, cowboy. Some of your moves are no doubt illegal in your home state."

He fought the urge to call bullshit. To do that meant to admit to too many things. Simpler to let her think she'd gotten away with her cover. "They passed a law special for me in Georgia and Tennessee."

The music began again, the lights dimming as the strains of "Talk Dirty to Me" by Poison started.

"Ready for more, or you done?"

"More," she said.

He had so many reasons he shouldn't, beginning and ending with the way his need strained the zipper of his trousers. Not when his body was howling for him to take her. *Take her. Plunge inside her. Make her scream and beg for you. Make her writhe until you are the one thing real in the world.*

He should walk away. Right now. He should tell her he was done with dancing. He longed to get the hell out of this place where the drumbeat of music called to him like an animal on the prowl. Dancing was so often a prelude to really good sex, with the rhythm of the music and their bodies writhing together creating its own sort of foreplay. Dancing with her was every bit the siren call he'd imagined it would be. Now here he was, and all he could think about was the way she would be under him instead of in front of him, her body flushed with desire.

Dirk cleared his throat, about to say, "Let's go." Then he took in her eager face and couldn't bring himself to disappoint her.

At least, that's what he told himself.

"All right, sunshine. I'm good for more."

****

Clubs were closing down when they left, the neon signs of the West Hollywood portion of Sunset Boulevard still flickering in Ally's vision. The few stars visible under the smog and lights shone in the sky. Cars still streamed in the road, heading various directions, some intent on additional partying, some going home.

His truck tires squealed as Dirk cut the curves too fast on the twisting, winding canyon road that led from Hollywood to the San Fernando Valley. A muscle was jumping at the back of his jaw.

All the conversational gambits she could think of fell flat in her mind before being spoken. She gazed out the window, contenting herself with his reflection in the glass. If she could just get home and shed this night, her reserve would reappear. Right now, she was on a knife-edge, need too strong within her, sliding through her defenses.

He slammed the pickup into park in her driveway, then turned to her.

She should jump out of the pickup and barricade herself in her room. She needed to hide under the covers until she stopped trembling and could control her longing for him.

"Do you want to come in for a nightcap?" she found herself asking instead, words coming to her through dense fog. His expression was dark, his jaw set. She needed to run her hands over his face, smooth out the hard lines, and kiss the tension away.

"Sure."

He followed her into the house, his boots loud in the quiet of the early hours. Ally tried not to think about the fact that the two of them were about to be alone.

She flipped on the overhead light, bathing them in its artificial glow, and went to the bar. "I've got vodka, scotch, and gin if nothing else is what you're after. Or beer. No Dixie, though." Did she sound normal? Reality was distant right now, and she had no way to tell.

"Scotch will do," he replied, stopping in the middle of the living room. The light rippled across his face.

She prepared a tumbler and handed it to him, then fled to the safety of the bar. She poured her own shot of vodka with shaking hands. He held the glass motionless before he downed half of it. His large body filled the room until he was all she could see. She swallowed hard and stepped out from behind the bar. She drank her shot quickly, the liquor burning as it went down. It warmed her, the alcohol radiating out and loosening her grip on her nerves. A faint trembling set in through her entire body, insistent desire making her knees loose.

"I...I had fun tonight," she said, aware that her voice was too high. She studied a spot on the far wall with fierce concentration. "Thanks."

Before she could even react, he had tossed the glass onto the couch. The remaining whiskey arced in the air as he strode across the room. Cupping her face and drawing her body to his, he kissed her. She opened to him without hesitation. His tongue drove inside her the way she sought his hardness to fit itself to her body.

Just one kiss. That should be all right.

She ran her fingers across his broad chest, marveling in the shudder of his frame, his slamming heartbeat, and the heat of his skin. His muscles rippled under her touch, and she stole her hands around his neck, stroking the skin there, filtering the silky strands of his hair through her fingers. He was a solid fixture in a world gone mad. She hung on, her breathing erratic. The soft hairs of his goatee brushed the sensitive skin of her cheeks, bringing nerve endings to life. She leaned into the kiss, meeting his thrust. The contact with his hard chest made her breasts swell. The tang of whiskey was sharp on her tongue. Cologne and sweat mingling together filled her nostrils.

She'd been aching for him for so long she was stunned she was in his arms. His kisses were ardent, the passion unmistakable. She didn't know what had changed.

The horrible truth dawned on her in the middle of the embrace. She'd been less than subtle at the Whammy Bar. He must have figured out she desired him and was acting on that. Gratitude drove him, not yearning. Men like him didn't covet women like her.

Pity. Poor Ally.

She pushed against his powerful chest, breaking the embrace. "Dirk, stop."

He did as she asked but made no move to release her. "Why?" he asked, baritone rough. His pulse beat hard and fast on his neck.

"I realize you're grateful." The idea of being out of his embrace was appalling. "I guess you must have gotten how much I desire you at the bar, but, Dirk, I don't need your pity."

His shocked exhalation made her dare to meet his gaze. His pupils had widened until a thin sliver of green was visible along the outside.

"Pity?" The word was harsh and much too loud. "Pity?" he repeated. "I'll show you pity." His hands shot down from her head, curved around her bottom, and he was tugging her to him again, stepping in to meet her at the same time he pulled her lower body flush with his.

Oh.

He ground his hips against hers, his manhood

straining. "Does that feel like pity?"

His body trembled, and she met his driving need with her own overwhelming desire. He was so aroused the beat of his private pulse slammed into her. His heartbeat started to race, and his breathing became erratic, matching the fierce, pulsing need unlike anything she'd ever felt.

Something long buried tore free inside her, and she turned her head up to his again. That primal expression he'd had earlier was on his face; now she understood what it meant. She was confident hers was similar.

"I'd very much like it," she said, her voice husky, "if you would kiss me again."

Okay, two kisses.

His full lips fitted themselves to hers as his tongue drove into her mouth. Her arms went around his neck again, and her hips moved against his. She twisted, her body burning, the shudder of his response flaming from within.

She hauled his shirt free from his pants, the heat of him coursing through her palms like an electric current. His skin rippled under her touch as she palmed the powerful muscles of his shoulders and the bones of his spine.

"Woman, we're going to burn this house down," he said when he lifted his head from hers.

"What a way to go." Her body trembled as her hips continued to move wildly.

He cupped her breasts, running his thumbs over her. She arched her back, her eyes closing from the exquisite torture of his fingers.

"Alanna," he said, his voice thick.

"Don't stop." She couldn't help the husky tone to

her voice. To her delight, he obeyed.

She shivered, sensations like slivers of glass pouring into her, threatening to shatter her. He transferred his mouth to her breast and shaped it. Her nipples stood out on the now-damp cloth, centers tightened to hard crests.

"You're beautiful." He played over the sensitive nerve endings as he talked.

She shuddered at the contact, digging her nails into his shoulders, holding on to the only thing real in this new universe. "I want you," she cried, her body quivering like a willow in an earthquake. Sensation poured through her with every beat of her heart, every tug of his mouth.

"I want you too," he said, his baritone harsh. "I'm on fire with it." He tugged her back into his arms again. This time his kiss was savage as he deepened the caress, tongue inside her mouth.

Nothing had ever been so good.

The smoky translucence of his gaze took in the shadowed cleft that lay between the top of her legs as her dress rode up. His large hand descended until it rested just below the hem. Dirk's thumb found her rising passion while his fingers curved over her curls. She moved over him, and he jerked in a motion that matched her arousal.

"Dirk, ah…" She pressed into the thumb threatening to shatter her to pieces.

"We need to stop." He smoothed her dress back over her hips. Stepping away from her hands, he took them in his own.

His passion was manifest in the shaking of his body and the fine sheen of arousal on his skin.

"Why?" she asked, echoing his words of earlier.

"Because." He stopped, his mouth moving. "Because," he said again, "you deserve love, a man who will stay and give you all the things you should have. I can't give you that. I shouldn't take you without that."

Words came to her slowly, her brain thick with the heady desire swamping her. She strung her sentences together with an effort as her body filled her with urgent demands. *Take his clothes off. Take your clothes off. Grab him and don't let him go.*

"I don't need love. That doesn't work for me." To her shock, it sounded believable. "Love is irrelevant. It's not for me. You are." Pride, caution, none of it mattered. She was drifting on a sea of elemental emotions, and no amount of dignity made any difference. She didn't care if he knew how much she wanted him—she had to try for this man or regret it the rest of her life.

She stepped back from him, reached down, grasped the hem of the dress, and drew it off. She pooled it up and let it slide to the floor. Her bra followed. "I don't care what form it takes—I have to have you. Please." She couldn't look at him. If he rejected her, she didn't know how she was going to be able to face him again.

"I...I shouldn't, but I can't say no. Not to you—to this. I'll give you what I can while I'm here, I promise. Is it enough?" Before she spoke, he was touching her again, thumb and forefingers rolling her nipples. His tongue followed, fire in its wake.

"It's enough," she managed before words became impossible. The assaults of fingers on both breasts and tongue moving in between had her shivering, head tossed back, hair draping as she arched her back. His relentless caresses lit her on fire with each deep tug of his tongue, each roll of his fingers. She dug her hands into the broad muscles of his shoulders, her nails biting his skin. Her breath caught on a series of thready, choppy gasps. She became a quivering bundle of sensation that was dissolving around her as the world transformed.

He stopped, took her body weight, and drew her up until her legs were around him. Kissing her, he held her still as his sex thrust against hers. She could scent her own desire and hoped he could as well. A broken cry escaped his lips. He kissed her again, holding her to his broad form.

"Bedroom, now, before I take you on the floor."

Chapter Fourteen

The flare of a match led to a soft candle flame, the only illumination in an unlit space. Lavender scent filled the room as the dim light danced on the walls. Gray slices of moonlight shone in through a shade that was half raised. Crickets chirped their mating dance outside. Somewhere in the distance was a yip of a dog or coyote.

Dirk was undressing while Ally lit the candle, his movements impatient as he struggled to be rid of his clothes. When he was done, he hooked his fingers under her panties and pushed them down, muttering under his breath when they caught on her thighs.

"Let me," she whispered. He braced her from behind as she stood on one foot to free first one leg from the confining garments, then the second. Then they were gone, discarded next to his larger clothes. Once she was naked, she began to turn around, but he kept her where she was, her back to his chest.

He couldn't stop the shuddering of his body or the rapid rise and fall of his chest. Nor could he control the slamming of his heart. Her body was trembling too—a miracle so great he sent his prayers up to his god. His manhood pressed into the small of her back, its hunger its own thing.

"Give me a minute," he rasped.

Resting her head on him, she reached behind and

began stroking his thighs with gentle, long caresses. A husky groan escaped his lips at her caress. Dirk brushed a kiss over the top of her head, his movements unsteady.

"I could come right now." He swallowed hard.

He shifted her to taste her mouth. The only way to keep from taking her too soon was to take it slow—if he could manage that.

He met her lips, opening her mouth to his, his tongue advancing and retreating while he continued to hold her. Then he slid his hands over her breasts, skin on skin, and was gratified when she gasped.

"Woman, you set me on fire." One hand went to her thatch of curls, and the other remained at her breast. She writhed at his ministrations, making him groan. She slid a hand between their bodies and grasped him at the base. He jerked at the contact, his breathing becoming even more ragged as she played over his length.

"Stop," he begged, moving to cover her hand with his, halting her, then moving her away from his body. "Stop, or this is going to end real fast." He turned her around, dragging her to him as his mouth descended to hers.

He bent over her with one arm around her waist. Then he shifted, tumbling them to the bed. Ally was flat underneath him, caught between him and the blankets covering her mattress. He kissed her in a slanting motion, plundering her mouth. She slid her arms around his back, scoring his flesh with her nails as she went.

He went still at the sensation, yanking his mouth from hers. Resting his head against hers, he fought to control his need. He whispered words but couldn't have said their meaning.

"Dirk?" Her lips feathered across his cheek in a soft caress. Then she buried her fingers in his hair, spearing through it to the hard muscles of his neck.

"Stop, oh God, stop," he begged. "It's just…give me a minute," he repeated. His baritone sliced through the air. A ragged sigh escaped him.

He couldn't control the ripples or the bead of moisture at the tip of him. He tried thinking of baseball, the Falcons, and paperwork, but all he could contemplate was the woman under him.

She cupped his butt. "Dirk, don't you see? I've longed for you for forever. I've dreamed of you the way you are right now, craving me so much you can't stand it. The fact that you do… Please…take me. Now."

She reached for the nightstand and opened a drawer. Desire was a raging inferno inside him. He was too close, his need too strong. One wrong move, and it would be over. She pressed something into his hand. A packet. He stared at it.

"They're two years old," she said. "I think they're still good. I can't be without you one second longer. Please. Take me. Now."

He was used to having to reassure his lovers that he would be gentle. Conscious of his size, he had always controlled his desires, careful not to reveal the naked heat of his full passion.

He focused on her. Nobody had ever sought the form of Dirk that was served up raw, a man as basic as it got.

Until now. He saw the desire in her. Desire for him. Everything he could give her.

She slid her arms around him again, reached up, and hauled his head down to hers. Whispering an elemental command, she bit his ear at the same time.

The dark words and the nip of her teeth stripped him of what little control he still had. He ripped apart the packet and got the condom on. His touch was less than gentle when he urged her legs open. He wasn't smooth as he entered her, almost pounding into her. She was tight, hot, and all female. Her body was slick with sweat, matching the heat of desire from him.

Slow down, damn it. Slow down.

They both watched as he slid inside her and back out again, as she met his thrusts with a jerk of her hips. Dirk shivered, body clenching, fighting not to end it right here.

Alanna raked his shoulders with her nails again.

Yes.

She cried out when he entered her. His primal side felt a circle had been completed—as if his other half had come home. The feel, the scent, the touch of her was spinning his world on its axis, making a mockery of anything being real besides her. Legs high around his, she took everything he could give her.

Resting his head on his forearm, he thrust into her, then slid down her slick body. She shuddered as he continued his relentless caress. She rocked against him, his name a broken cry.

"Sweet Jesus."

Uttering a harsh rasp, he gathered her to him, so close she was almost part of him. They pulsed and danced hotly together. Release raged over him.

When he finally started to surface, they were still wrapped up together, the edge of hunger abating but not gone.

But the pain was.

****

Dirk made a movement as if to push out of her. Ally murmured a protest, her arms and legs twined with his.

"I'm crushing you," he said without moving.

They still lay naked on top of her mound of blankets. Who needed a blanket when she had her own personal six-feet-five heater? A square patch of moonlight fell across the bed, touching him with its gray beams.

"Cowboy, I'm not very crushable." She savored his arms around her, his legs twined with hers, but most of all the stunning reality of him still inside her.

He did move then, leaning over to turn on the nightstand lamp. Shifting so he could raise himself up on his elbow, he studied her. His unkempt hair fell across his face. With an impatient gesture he flipped it to the left where it covered one eye.

He tilted her head up. "You need to stop running yourself down. Let me tell you something about the woman in this bed. She's got incredible curves, broad shoulders, and hips that a man can hang on to. She fills my palm when I cup her butt, and her breasts spill over me when I touch them. She's a woman who doesn't make me feel so gigantic. You fit me. With you I'm not gonna break something."

She stroked his face with a gentle hand, the stubble of his five-o'clock shadow under her palm. His words warmed her in parts of her she hadn't been aware were cold until now.

"Thanks." She traced the outline of his lips with her index finger. The soft kiss he pressed against her finger thrilled her. "I'll try to stop the pity parade. I can't guarantee I won't relapse, but I'll try."

The emerald of his gaze was so bright her lashes fell under the heat of his stare.

"I wish you saw what I do. I shouldn't have to remind you how beautiful you are. I can't imagine how I kept away from you for so long."

She searched his eyes and couldn't make out anything but earnest truth. "How long have you fancied me?"

He snorted at the deliberately used word but didn't comment on it. "Since before I knew your name at the bar. You?"

All this time he had been grappling with the same emotions. Even though she'd just sworn to Dirk to stop feeling sorry for her, she figured he hadn't been attracted to her from the start. She told herself it had been time and proximity that shifted his emotions. She had not expected to hear that he wanted her from the beginning. Ally wasn't the type for love at first sight. That was how her life went.

"I guess I knew your name already, because Gordon had introduced us, but pretty much the same."

"Really?" His mouth opened in surprise. "You mean all this time I've hated myself for measuring you for a Dirk suit, you desired me all along?"

"That's the truth. You're magnificent," she said. "Someone ought to sculpt you. Or bottle you."

"Yeah?" Flipping his hair back, he perused her form. He was hardening again as he surveyed her. "Someone should paint you, naked in a field of wildflowers. Then again, I don't want anyone else appreciating what I've got. They get a gander at your gorgeous curves, and I'll be fighting duels all the time. I can't have guys viewing my woman that way."

The matter-of-fact summation startled her. "Is that what I am? Your woman?"

His goatee tugged down when he frowned, making him so ferocious that he might be scary if he hadn't just made sweet love to her. "If you're plannin' on dating guys, forget it. I don't share."

Her lips curved up at his dour words. The possessiveness in his voice was unlike anything she'd ever heard before. "Mercy, Dirk, you trying to kill me? You're all any woman can manage."

He leaned over her. His hair fell across his neck again, framing his face. "Good. I don't believe in going with more than one person at a time. You may as well get that I've got a possessive streak. Since I can't have my woman macking on new dudes, it's fair I do the same."

She smothered a laugh, tilting her head back. "An alpha male and a possessive streak? Dirk, I'm disappointed. That's close to being a cliché."

He growled, a feral low hum that emitted from the back of his throat. A growl that sent every erogenous zone in her body racing with desire.

"You'll pay for that," he promised, pressing a kiss to her forehead.

"I was counting on it."

He kissed her eyelids, the lashes surrounding them, and the space in between. Then he touched her high cheekbones and feathered a kiss at the tip of her nose. He grasped her hair and tugged, arching her head back.

Instead of her lips, he kissed the indentation in the middle of her chin before trailing lower, across her neck. He bent to press his lips on the bones in the

165

column she bared to him. Then he kissed her with rising hunger, his tongue thrusting hard into her mouth. She responded with the wild passion called from within her. She began stroking his back again with long caresses, nails scoring his skin with her movements.

"One of the best things about being naked with a woman is the heat of her body and the warmth of her skin. I may never have mentioned it," he said, shoving his hair behind his ear when it tumbled forward again, "but I love being petted. You're lighting me on fire right now. Touch me anywhere, anytime. Could be a problem in the office since I'm gonna think about throwing you across my desk and taking you if you do, but never feel like you can't touch me."

Her body tightened at the idea of the two of them locked in his office, her on top of his desk, him inside her. The remnants of Connor's old rejections fell away. "Thanks. I may have to take you up on that. The desk part sounds good too. Thanks for everything."

"I've got you, girl. I'm not going to let you fall." He was silent for a moment. "The first time was so fast. I felt savage, like an animal. You didn't mind?"

She pretended to consider, her lips twitching with suppressed amusement. "Hmm. I guess I'm going to have to up the volume on those moans of ecstasy, since you didn't hear them the first time. Me, I believe the guys in the next county could."

A short laugh escaped him, and he drew her to him again. "You've got a pert mouth, miss." Mirth danced across his face. "I like it. I think it's payback time now, Missy Alanna, so you may as well lie back and enjoy it. I've been longing to know all this time if you taste good, and I'm gonna find out now." His eyes held a hard edge of lust.

"If I don't lie back?"

Twirling a nonexistent moustache, he lowered his voice to the very bottom of its register. "I have my ways."

This playful quality was unexpected in a man that most assumed stern at best and dour at worst.

"Well, then, I have no choice, do I? You might tie me to the tracks if I resist. Those railroad ties are dirty." She reclined, arms stretched over her head to better show off her bosom, until her entire body was open for his perusal.

His lashes swept down to follow his gaze as he took in the bones of her hips, then across her sex, down her thighs and calves. Then he reversed his direction, heading back up to play his gaze over her. He acted as if he were a starving man who was being offered a steak dinner with potatoes and all the sides.

"Has there been anyone since Belinda?"

His head jerked up to meet her gaze. He nodded, making his hair wave in a cascading motion. She tried not to be perversely disappointed.

"There were a few after the divorce. Not many. None of them caught fire. With Belinda, the last year we didn't make love much. After the scandal and before the divorce, we stopped being intimate. I should have known she was leaving, but it still surprised me that she did. I would have stayed faithful to her forever—would have adjusted to a passionless marriage if that's what it took. She didn't stay. She did me a favor. Even in Nashville not everyone knew, or cared, about what I was accused of. Not many, though, Alanna. Not many."

His expression shuttered, and she was sorry she'd

said anything.

"Now, I just don't get what Belinda was thinking. I can't imagine how anyone could be naked in the same bed with you and keep their hands off you. As for the silly women in Nashville, that's their loss—my gain."

He grunted, and she couldn't tell if the sound meant amusement or melancholy.

"Come here," she continued. "I have to kiss you. Now."

When he hovered over her, frozen, she gripped his head, biting his lips until his tongue slid between hers. Then he pushed her onto the mattress, tongue thrusting inside her in a furious frenzy of need as he aligned his body with hers.

"Alanna," he said when he broke away, his voice hoarse. "The second time shouldn't be like the first. It should last. I craved nothing more than licking every inch of your body until you were crying for me. I wanted to make me the one thing real in your universe. It's been a hell of a long time since I've needed someone the way I need you."

She emitted a sigh of relief that he was back with her. Leaning back again, she was careful not to touch him. "No need to tell me what you were thinking. Show me."

"I would start by tracing your face." He brushed his fingers across the lines of her forehead, her cheeks, and the curve of her lips. Then he cupped her jaw, long fingers on the length of her neck while the second laced in her hair, urging her head back. "Then I would plant kisses across it." His breath was hot when he placed butterfly kisses across her cheeks. "For weeks I tried to think of ways to touch you so I could determine if your skin was soft and if you were sensitive at the base of your neck."

Her heartbeat increased when he nipped her. His tongue slid over her collarbone again, pausing right above the V to brush a caress there. His beard stubble rasped against her skin, an incredible pleasure/pain in a body gone hot with desire.

"I could barely sleep at the idea of touching your breasts." He adjusted his hands, fitting them to her. He was staring at their joined bodies, rapture on his features.

"Dirk?" she asked.

"Mine," he growled. "All mine." He stroked her with his thumbs until the small centers were hard pebbles under his touch. She moaned, moving restlessly against him, desire shooting through her like strings of a guitar.

He bent his head and touched one nipple with his tongue, then drew it inside his mouth. He repeated the action on the remaining breast, laving them with his mouth until he was biting them while his tongue played out over the hard nubs. He kissed underneath them, flicking over her aching nipples. Then moved his arms under her shoulders, lifting her for his mouth, arching her back until she was bent to him, her body bowed.

She cried out again, insistent desire once again gripping her in its throes. She twisted, trying to bury herself in his potent male body.

"You turn on hotter and faster than any woman I've ever met," he growled, releasing her so he could move lower, his breath on her belly. "You taste better than I could ever have imagined." He kissed her ribcage, then his tongue stabbed at her navel, a caress that made her jerk in unexpected pleasure. She had to release his head and grasped his shoulders, her body undulating, her nails digging into him. Then he was moving down, placing warm kisses on her, his hair trailing across her as well, itself a sensual weapon.

"I want…" she began, but she had no words for her desire, just an overpowering need for this man.

"I know what I'm after. You—all of you." He slid his fingers into her waiting arousal.

She arched into his hand, hips writhing.

"Alanna, let me love you. All of you."

He released her and then laced their fingers together, holding them joined next to her hips. His head was just above her sex, then his mouth was against her. She shuddered, shifting to give him full access. She gave herself to him, her body on a rack of desire. She fell, his name on her lips, her hips moving helplessly, and she once again came apart in his arms.

She collapsed back on the bed, and he was reaching for the nightstand, pulling out a packet, rolling it onto him, and then driving into her willing body. He pressed her back, thrusting all the way to his hilt, then urging her legs around his torso.

He was buried inside her, all he could give her, and she took it all gladly. He stared at her flushed, naked body and grunted.

"Don't know where I stop and you begin," he said. "Heaven." He began moving.

He bent down to kiss her, his harsh cry muffled by her mouth. He tore the contact away and stretched out, his teeth drawn back in a grimace as his big body jerked, coming to her again. She cried out, a short, surprised yelp as she reached her climax a second time.

The room shattered around them as he drove into her one final time, his body rigid, the white-hot incandescence of their mutual passion burning to her core.

Chapter Fifteen

Dirk eased out of her bed and slipped on his jeans. He padded out of the bedroom and stared at the closed second room where the mom cat and her kittens were. He liked cats just fine but preferred dogs. Mutts could go on a fishing trip and help with catching the salmon. They could flush out deer and wildlife. He hadn't had a dog since he moved to Nashville, but his parents had a series of dogs that he got to visit with when he went home. It didn't matter. No animals for him. Not right now. A pet signaled permanence. That wasn't Dirk and sure as heck wasn't Los Angeles.

She said the cats were rescues, but he'd seen the way she beheld the black-and-white kitten. He doubted that cat was going anywhere besides Alanna's home.

Lucky cat. She would tend to its needs before her own, just like she did everything else. When she committed to something, she saw it through.

He retrieved his cell phone from his jacket and thumbed through the messages. One from his brother. He checked the time. Going on five a.m. It would be eight o'clock at his brother's place—late enough to call. He'd been in this place three months. While it might not be as bad as he'd first feared, California wasn't for him. He had a plan, and no gorgeous blonde should derail it.

He ignored the nagging part of him that told him

otherwise.

His phone beeped with a text. He frowned at it. Ryder. That was odd. Hoss had to know the hour. He stared at the phone. He shouldn't be jealous of Ryder, but the man had just spent several days in the same city as Alanna and had even taken her to some crazy bat thing under a bridge in Austin. Ryder was a good man and wouldn't poach if Dirk had a claim.

Did he, though? Have the right to Alanna?

—What's up?—

Ryder's reply was quick.

—Sorry, didn't realize the time.—

—I reckon not. What's on your mind, Ry?—

—This may not be my place, but…—

—Out with it, Ry. Just spit out the chew before it chokes you.—

—All right. Don't let that woman slip away, or you'll regret it.—

Dirk was going to reply with something smart-ass but then let his fingers fall from the keys. What little he learned about Ryder was enough to recognize the man had a past—he just didn't talk about it. Like men should.

—Noted, hoss. Anything else before I commune with the chickens?—

He could almost sense Ryder smiling. The man had been a good friend to him, and he deserved to be treated that way.

—Naw. That'll do for now. You take care of her, you hear?—

—I will. Thanks. It's…complicated.—

—Women always are.—

A meow from the second room reminded him that

the cats were in there. Then the door moved as scratching started on the other side. He glanced toward Alanna's bedroom. Faint mews emitted from beyond the door. They must have heard his big feet and responded.

The scraping became more insistent. Finally, he used his feet to block the door before sliding inside and shutting the door behind him.

The mom cat tilted up her head when he came in. The black-and-white kitten that was Alanna's favorite wasted no time in hopping up his jeans with its razor-sharp claws to reach the big man. He plucked the scamp up by the scruff of the neck and carried him to his face. The beast mewed at him and batted his nose, grazing it with his sharp claws.

He might not be a cat person, but this was Alanna's rescue kitty, and that made the difference. The kit kneaded on his bare arm and then tried to suckle him. He gave the cat a pat and set him down by his mother. The black-and-white marauder launched itself onto his jeans again, beginning the climb up.

"All right, you little rascal." He removed the creature from his pants before he could leave any more tears in his flesh. He petted the baby for a minute before setting it down and easing out before the kitten could make its way across the floor again.

He needed to call Greg back. He cast another glance to where the delicious Alanna was still sleeping, one arm thrown over the pillows as though she wasn't used to sharing her bed. A frisson of pleasure speared him. He was glad she hadn't had any recent bed partners. It made their union that much sweeter.

He could not think this way. Would not think this

way. This was no basic cable TV movie where love conquered all. His sole purpose in coming here was to get back to Nashville, or home, when he could. No Yankee was going to change that.

No matter how delicious she was to kiss. To have sex with. Dirk frowned. What they were doing went beyond sex. Her honey-sweet scent, clean like the flower blossoms in springtime, was an achingly familiar aroma. The way she took care of things, without fuss, harkened him back to his early days, before life had gone haywire.

She was more woman than he'd expected to find. She reminded him of home.

No. She was not. Georgia was home. Alanna was a waystation.

With that uppermost in his mind, he called his brother.

Later, Alanna had the kitten on the sofa and was playing with it.

"I got to admit that's a cute cat."

She was using a modified fishing pole, and the beast was chasing it around. Dirk grunted with laughter as he watched them. Then the kitten tuckered out and crawled into her lap where it fell asleep, paws akimbo. The sight of her with a defenseless creature in her lap made his skin tighten. The curve of her back and head as she leaned toward the critter reminded him of how his mother cared for him when he was small. Her blonde hair swung forward, half blocking her face.

"The rescue found them in the middle of the road in a bag. Someone tossed them out, expecting them to be run over. When they got the babies, the poor mama was skin and bones from trying to feed all five," she said. "There are times when I hate humanity. They allow a cat to get pregnant when there are all sorts of programs. Then they toss the kittens into the street to die. What kind of person are they?"

He answered, despite understanding she'd asked a rhetorical question. "Sometimes they drown them. Or shoot them."

"Either would have been kinder if the right person hadn't been in the right spot that day. I'm a realist. I'm aware of what goes on in this world. I can't save them all. Nature is harsh, and that's the truth. What bothers me is the casual cruelty of man." The kitten made a contented sound, and she turned back to it, stroking it under the chin.

He couldn't help but gaze at her, thinking of all the ways she cared for the beings in her life, from the tiniest animal to the biggest man. He desired nothing more than to stretch out like the cat had and allow her to tend to him. He would find it far too easy to bask in Alanna's presence. For eternity.

That brought him up short. He fought the feelings back down, unable to stop them from tumbling within him.

"You're giving me the weirdest face. What is it?"

"You will make a great mother," he said, his baritone a rumble in the air.

Out of nowhere the image coalesced. A six-month-old baby lying in her arms suckling. Sandy blond hair was on his head, his size already speaking of a large frame, and the promise of green eyes under the baby blue.

"Thanks," she said. "Many disagreed with you on that score. Anyway, it's a long way off. I'm a little old fashioned in that regard. I'd like the husband and the ring first."

Things he couldn't offer her. Things she deserved.

Things she had never expressed any interest in getting from him. She was warm and passionate, but he had never seen her yearn for more than they had.

"You deserve that, Alanna, and more."

"It's funny. When I was with Connor, I didn't want kids, but he was obsessed with the idea that I was going to get pregnant and trap him into marriage. Still, he hated condoms. He left that to me. I got sick once, and he was so worried I was pregnant—morning sickness. He didn't know the difference between the flu and that."

She got up, and the kitten protested. She carried him to the spare room where the kittens were meowing and tumbling around. She placed the critter on the floor. He tried to dash out, but she shut the door before he could.

Dirk heard meowing through the closed door before it stopped.

He knew how the beast felt. Once Alanna started petting him, he never wanted it to stop. She slid her now-free arm around Dirk, holding him close before she settled back into his lap, this time on the couch. A peaceful lassitude took him when her breath sighed over him as he held her. She ran her hands over his hair in a stroking motion, lighting his body on fire in its wake.

He wasn't sure if a minute, an hour, or an eternity went by before they moved again.

"You are the only woman I've ever met who values silence as much as words." He wondered at the expression on her face.

"I think that's a compliment, so, thanks? I think?"

"You're gonna keep that one."

She murmured a protest and settled in his arms again. "I haven't decided anything. Kittens are easy to find homes for."

"Naw. You're keeping him. What are you going to name him?"

"Dirk!" She smacked at him and then smoothed her hand over the spot. "Too soon, cowboy. I have to admit that you may be right. May being the operative word. I'm thinking Patches if he winds up a permanent resident. I'd keep the mom too if I did. She'll be harder to place."

Her satisfied smirk reminded him of his early days with Belinda before things went bad. She had the assured grin of a woman who already knew her mind but wasn't about to tell her man that.

Her man. *Damn it.* He had no business thinking that.

To cover, he coughed and slid her off his lap. "Let's get this show on the road. We got chores to do. Come on. Time to take a shower." He arched one eyebrow, unable to keep the need from his voice. "Then I'll dry you off," he said, baritone rumbling. "But not with a towel."

****

He loves me.

He loves me not.

He definitely loves me not.

You are an idiot.

"Ally. Ally!"

Gordon rapped his knuckles three times on her

desk before she came out of her wool gathering.

"Oh, hi, Gordon." She shifted some papers around, trying to make it seem like she wasn't just staring at the computer. "What can I... How can I help you?"

"You're friends with that gal over at Apposite, so maybe you already heard."

Gordon said "gal over at Apposite" with such a dismissive air that Ally didn't follow what he said for a minute. Then she realized he was talking about Terri. "Oh—Terri. We're friends, but we haven't talked this week. What's up?" She didn't mention the night at the Whammy Bar and the things Harris had said. She should have called Terri before now. She would rectify that soon.

He looked as though he didn't believe her, but then he just shrugged. "They're in trouble. They might go under. Get ready because we could be bringing another catalog in if we win the bidding."

Great. More items to manage. She riffled through her projects in her mind and sighed. She already had a full plate, but she wouldn't say no.

She never did.

"How many titles? Apposite doesn't have much in the way of a marketing department, so would we be talking about a relaunch? Or just absorbing the catalog into our own?"

"I'm not sure yet. Check out the catalog when you get a chance and give me your opinion as soon as you can. I've got Dirk on Jess, so you can focus on this."

She absorbed what Gordon was saying, trying not to let the dismay show on her face. "You're taking me off Jess? To examine a potential catalog we might not even buy?" The words were out before she could stop them. She was flabbergasted at the suggestion.

He raised his hands, his expression swinging from neutral to surprised, perhaps at her speaking up at all. Ally was the one who did whatever the company needed. Everyone knew that.

"No, no, sorry I misspoke. I just… You have a lot going on. I figured I'd take something off your plate if you had too much going on."

"Jess is my artist. Dirk and I are doing it together." If Gordon learned the truth, it would be disastrous. They hadn't talked about it, but she assumed that Dirk had the good sense to keep what was going on between themselves.

She would have to talk to him about that. While she didn't consider him to be the enemy anymore, he was still in her way. She hadn't yet figured out how to reconcile the two.

Anyway, he wasn't staying. He'd made that clear. The question was moot.

"Okay, good." She wouldn't raise her hand to her cheek to check the temperature. That would show weakness in a way she didn't allow. Not since the kids. "I'll give it a once-over. The catalog, that is. It's no more than a couple of dozen titles, right?"

Gordon swallowed, his face shifting back toward relieved. "Something like that."

"Is this public knowledge? Can I talk to Terri about it, or would you prefer I keep it to myself? What about…" She paused, not sure if saying Dirk's name would make it obvious, but then just forged ahead. "Dirk?"

"Dirk should be brought into the loop. I'll have a soft copy of the files sent to you. We will need to move fast. Earthy Cry and many indie labels are also going to bid. That's what I hear. As for your friend, if you can get any inside scoop, do it. She shouldn't be loyal to Apposite now that she is losing her gig."

She considered Terri and the idea that she might lose her job. She'd have to check if she was going to be okay. Not that Ally had oodles of cash lying around, but she did have a house if… She broke off that thinking. She had to get out of the habit of attempting to rescue people before they asked.

Gordon seemed to take her silence for assent. "The files will be there shortly. While you're doing your part, I'll have the finance guys run the numbers."

"Sure."

He opened his mouth to say more but then nodded before retreating from her office.

She sat there for a minute until her email dinged with an incoming message. Gordon's initial words echoed through her mind. *I've got Dirk on Jess.* He must have misspoken. Yes, Dirk had come in at a higher position than Ally—the one she coveted—but Gordon couldn't be suggesting moving her off her projects. The fact that he backed down showed that.

Gordon wouldn't assign her the grunt work and give all the good stuff to Dirk. Would he?

She'd never said no to anything. She'd always done what Gordon asked even if it went against her own self-interests. She was a pushover, and everyone knew it.

She needed to change that.

Chapter Sixteen

Drumming her fingers on the table, Ally examined the room. The only occupants were her, Jess, Dirk, and the video conference equipment. Jess sat in front of a laptop, her head framed in the video conference window.

After two days of endless calls, Ally was bored. Jess had to wow radio on a minuscule budget, and by that count the virtual trip had been a raging success. Radio executives were falling victim to her sassy charm. The interviews and on-camera offers she'd received made everything worthwhile.

Ally was comfortable with silence. She'd always believed she was a loner, but being with Dirk had made a mockery of that idea. She separated a lock of her hair and twined her fingers around the wave. She'd indulged the habit when she was younger and, now that her hair was longer, picked it up again. She dropped her hand, focusing on their artist.

Gordon beckoned to her, and she exited the room. Dirk watched her as she did so, and she flashed him a grin over her shoulder. His eyes darkened and went smoky before he gave her a thumbs-up.

She wondered if they were fooling those around them or if everyone realized what was going on. Ally wasn't that close to her co-workers, and extricating herself from their events in favor of Dirk hadn't proved too difficult. Most only cared about a person when they were standing in front of them. That might be cynical, but that didn't stop it from also being the truth.

"What's up, Gordon?"

He had an aggrieved expression as he leaned against the wall, facing her. "Forget about Apposite's catalog. Earthy Cry swooped in and outbid the rest of us. Apposite is folding. We're grabbing Kai Halara to help with Jess' upcoming tour, but everyone else is being let go. You can stop analyzing the titles and call your friend. Pump her for information. She might have nuggets nobody else has."

She absorbed the news, rocking back on her heels. The door was closed to the conference room, but she could still hear the faint voices of the radio executives and Jess talking as the interviews progressed. "Why Kai? What is he going to do? Why wouldn't he go to Earthy Cry?"

Gordon shrugged. "I haven't the faintest idea. He was available, so we took him to manage Jess' tour. We needed a manager, and he used to do that before he started in the record business. He's a little rusty, but he's also cheap. Like so many labels we're doing this on a shoestring. I'm sure your friend is a good employee, but we don't need her. She'll find something. Check into what you can find out about the company. Maybe there's still wiggle room with the catalog."

She wasn't aware she was going to say the words until she spoke them. "I'm not going to do that."

He blinked. She waited, needing to say more but forcing herself to stay silent.

"What did you say?" Gordon's tone indicated that

he expected her to take her words back.

She clung to every ounce of her newfound resolve not to start jabbering. The murmur of voices was still evident through the door. She longed to jab her finger at Gordon, but he was still her boss.

"I'm not going to spy for you. My spying days are done. All of them."

She tossed her hair, wishing she'd gotten it longer so it would have a more dramatic impact. Her heart was pounding, the blood rushing so loud in her ears it felt like she was at the ocean.

"You work for me."

She raised her chin, reviewing her bank account. She wouldn't last long without employment. Her mortgage took a large chunk of her salary, even with Dad's hefty down payment, and she had the normal living in Los Angeles expenses.

Panic welled inside her, and she fought to keep it down. Her usual modus operandi would be to give in.

"I do, but that doesn't mean I sell out my beliefs. I do my job and far over that as well. I'm done gathering dirt for you."

Her backup plan, to determine if Terri had any work she could do, was out the window. She'd picked the worst possible time to take a stand. She stood there, willing her knees to stop shaking, praying her rising fear didn't show.

"Well, fuck," Gordon swore.

She didn't trust her voice to words, so she just stared.

He must have interpreted that as a challenge because his nostrils flared, and his lips thinned. "Fine." He sounded aggrieved and stepped away from her as he spoke. "Hell of a time for you to grow a spine. Get things ready for Kai Halara. You may as well do what I pay you for."

Unsure whether she would be fired or not, Ally swallowed and retreated.

Dirk gave her a questioning glance when she slipped back into the room, but she shook her head. The awareness of what just happened pounded through her. She never stood up for herself.

She tried to focus on the radio interviews even while the confrontation danced in her mind. Had she just told Gordon no? Was she free of spying on Dirk?

Perhaps, perhaps not. She was going to behave as though she was.

She almost whistled before she remembered Jess was on calls. She had agreed to things that went contrary to her nature out of fear, but she was going to work on that. She did her job, and she was damned good at it. That should be enough.

Now she had to hope Dirk would never find out what she had done.

She might tell him at some point. Although, by the time she did, she doubted it would be relevant.

In the meantime, tonight was the Attraction show. She'd told Terri she would go, despite her misgivings about Clarke Masters, and she wasn't about to renege on a promise.

When they got there, she searched for Terri but couldn't find her friend. Ally and Dirk had access passes, but she wasn't about to go to the backstage and look for Terri. Terri might have forgiven Clarke for what happened ten years earlier, but Ally wasn't there yet. Plus, she didn't want to engage Harris. Terri would emerge in due course.

As the show went on and her friend wasn't around, Ally tried to enjoy the performance but found herself checking her phone every few minutes. The Terri that she was friends with today—the reliable, stable Terri—would not just flake out on a gig. While Ally didn't understand all the details of her current relationship with Clarke Masters, the singer of Attraction and Terri's long-ago crush, she was aware they were dating. She could tell Terri was head over heels for him.

Ally wasn't sure how she felt about that, but she couldn't make that call. Clarke was the man who tripped Terri's triggers. That made one of them.

She checked her phone again. No texts.

Clarke was strutting around the stage with every inch of his old swagger. His hair was shorter than it had been in pre-modern days, and his face showed the years, but overall he was the same. What had he done? Ally was sure he was responsible for Terri's disappearance.

She didn't like him. He had treated Terri abominably and had been a wreck of a human being back then. She reminded herself that this was Terri's relationship and not hers, but she couldn't help it. The man couldn't have changed that much.

Two calls were enough. Whatever was going on with Terri, she would get back to Ally when she was able. Then Ally would be as good a friend to Terri as she could be.

She wanted to leave but couldn't deprive Dirk of the pleasure of the night. They were backed into a corner of the VIP section, with Dirk against the outside wall. Ally stood in front of him, enjoying his warmth while they didn't quite touch. The air of the forbidden wasn't lost on her and lent a certain spice to the evening. She could feel his masculine heat and the magnetism that washed out of him in waves.

When the spotlight veered to them, Clarke pointed their direction. She wasn't sure if he recognized her or not, but he nodded toward them. Maybe. She wouldn't put it past Clarke to be fooling around with additional women while claiming to be involved with Terri. Time was when both women would have been overjoyed with that sort of attention, real or imagined.

Harris pointed to her and waved. She waved back. Dirk grunted, his hand on her back reminding her he was there. She needed no such prompt. No matter where she was, he was with her.

She was in love with Dirk.

The sheer folly of the recognition almost made her laugh. Of course, she was. She went from impossible man to impossible man. Dirk was just a new bead in the string. She should stick with guys like Harris—at least then she knew what she was getting.

Attraction started one of their most popular songs, and the crowd erupted. People tried to jockey for position and get closer to the stage, only to get pushed back by those in front. Ally longed to glance at her phone to find out the time but didn't. She would make it through this one minute at a time.

She wished Terri were there to give her an unbiased opinion. Everyone else was too close to the situation. She had been counting on introducing the two of them and getting Terri's take on Dirk. Terri was her friend, with shared history, and Ally could count on Terri's honest opinion.

The song ended, and a new one began. She'd done this sort of thing before, when she was dating Harris, and had gone to countless Attraction shows. No matter how good the music, hearing the same thing night after night got old.

She would endure.

She always did.

****

"Where's your friend?"

Dirk glanced around the club. He'd been hoping to meet Terri August. Of all Alanna's friends she was the one who was the most interesting. Their shared history made him long to quiz the woman until she spilled Alanna's secrets. He longed to learn every one of them.

Alanna was texting on her phone while also glancing around. "I can't find her. It's crazy in here, but regardless it's not a big club. Sooner or later, I should spot her. I don't think she's here, and she's not answering her cell."

"I got a half a foot or more on you, but I don't know what she looks like."

She frowned, and he stepped closer to her. If they hadn't been in the VIP section of the club, the crush would have been unbearable. Even that area was packed with folks waiting for the one-off return of the former superstar band Attraction.

"It's so weird."

Dirk had to crane his neck to hear Alanna.

"She was all aglow with excitement over tonight. Something must have happened." She tapped out a message and then glanced toward the backstage area. "I hate to disturb them, but I need to find Terri. I'll be back shortly."

He wanted to smooth her worry lines away but should keep his concern to himself. Their relationship was between themselves, and even though others speculated about their closeness, not a soul was aware of the truth.

Perhaps nobody except Terri. He wasn't sure. He yearned to take the measure of this old friend before determining if he could relax in her presence.

They were walking a fine line. Something was going to have to change. He glanced around the packed club, remembering similar events in his early years when he was building his reputation. Back then he would find promising bands and offer his services for free, just to get credibility. Those days should be long behind him, yet here he was.

Truth was the idea of striking out on his own again, not being beholden to anyone else, had a lot of appeal. Being here, in this club, reminded him of a time when things were new and everything hadn't gone to hell in a handbasket.

Maybe he couldn't do that in Nashville. Maybe he could. He didn't have a clear idea which way to go. Not with Alanna in the balance and his life shifting every time he went in a new direction.

"She's not here. Harris doesn't know where she is."

Alanna slid next to him, and his hand flexed with the urge to touch her. He couldn't do that, much as he craved it. He was afraid one of them would get tossed out on their ear if Gordon got wind of what was happening.

Besides, they would be home soon enough. Then she was his.

All his.

When the show was done, Dirk raised an eyebrow in the direction of the Whammy Bar right next door. "You hungry, darlin'? We can grab some grub before we call it a night. Unless you're too tired."

Ally gave another look around the rapidly emptying club and then heaved out a breath. "Sure. That's fine."

He pressed his hand to her back as they walked, searching for the words. He had so many things he wanted to say, and he wasn't going to say any of them.

They were getting seated, trailing the maitre d' as he escorted them to a table, when he heard the voice.

"Like a bad penny, Dirk Roberts turns up again."

Dirk's mouth flattened into a line, tension stiffening his spine, making his movements jerky.

Marlon was standing several feet away, talking to an unfamiliar person but staring at Dirk and Ally.

Red colored Dirk's vision. His gaze fixed on Marlon. "Didn't expect to find you here, Marlon." He gestured around the Hollywood eatery. He had begun to relax and maybe even enjoy Los Angeles when Marlon had to spoil it.

"The same."

Ally walked up to the short man, her eyes never leaving his as she approached. The person Marlon had been with took in the tableau and fell silent.

What the hell is she doing?

"Hello, Marlon." She offered her hand to the man.

Dirk kept a close watch on the proceedings. If he had to physically remove her, he would.

"We've met before. I'm Ally Wilson." She was smiling, but any fool could make out the anger simmering behind her face.

She was magnificent.

"I'm aware of who you are, ma'am." He touched his hat but made no move to take her hand. "I believed you'd have better sense than to continue to associate with this guy."

White teeth flashed in a feral gleam. She had no welcome or laughter behind the smile, which was predatory instead of calming. "Guess I'm like Dirk, Marlon—I don't learn my lessons worth a damn."

Dirk stayed close to her, wishing she wouldn't cause a scene but also glorying in it.

"Guess not." His gaze went to Dirk and then back to Ally.

His associates shifted in their seats. Dirk hadn't seen Marlon at the show, but that didn't mean he hadn't been there. Or maybe he'd been at one of the clubs in the area. Anything was possible.

"Were you at the Attraction gig? Dirk and I didn't see you there."

Marlon raised his head, sniffing dismissively. "We had an artist doing a showcase nearby, so I stopped in. That brand of rock and roll is past its prime."

Dirk met Alanna's gaze, wondering what she was up to. He yearned to yank her back from the table, but he knew better than to crowd a woman when she was angry. Her hazel eyes were the color of cold rain, her features arranged in set lines.

"You missed a good show." Dirk growled out the words.

Alanna snorted at his statement, and Dirk tilted his head. So many things were happening at once he was trying to make sense of them.

"Did I? I am sure they will launch some pathetic reunion tour now. Clarke Masters is an addict, and he can't be trusted. Like some others." Marlon's tight tone was every bit as venomous as Dirk's rumble.

The tableau of the three of them must have been a sight. The tall man with a beautiful woman next to him who was facing a man her height with fury written across every line of her body screamed of a real interesting backstory to even the most casual of observers. He was aware of the silence around them even if she wasn't. Many folks had turned to the group with curious gazes. Romans at the forum. Christians against the lions. Thumbs up or thumbs down?

"I guess they might go on tour. The crowd was into it. Anything is possible." Ally's smile didn't reach her eyes.

"They sold out an eight-hundred-capacity club. It's not exactly the Grand Ole Opry." Marlon flicked a hand toward the direction of the club as though in dismissal.

"It's a start." She appeared like she was going to say more but then closed her mouth.

When the silence lingered, Dirk bumped her with his hand.

Her fists were clenched at her sides, and her attention never lifted from Marlon. "You have a lot of opinions. I've got some too."

"Course you do, little lady. Why don't you mosey on away from the table and let us enjoy our evening?" His attention went from Alanna to Dirk and back to Alanna. "You ought to be careful in your associations. Folks might get the wrong idea."

She paused, and Dirk fought not to yank her away.

"Is that so? Huh. Thanks for the advice. I doubt I'll

take it. I don't usually pay heed to supreme assholes."

Both men jerked in surprise. Hearing the harsh swears from her mouth sent a shaft of satisfaction through Dirk.

"Aw, come now, is this about the Apposite catalog? I heard Shatter Sound was trying to nose in. No need to get twisted. It's just business."

Dirk could almost feel Alanna vibrate with anger. He wasn't sure he'd ever caught her temper. She was so easygoing, taking everything in stride and never letting things ruffle her. This surprised him—in the very best of ways.

"I guess that's right. It's all corporate intrigue. Sharks in the water. Kill or be killed."

"Yep." Marlon raised his hand as though he was going to adjust his hat but then let it fall.

"I'm a Northerner. East Coast born and bred. I knew diddly-squat about the South until I met all you guys. Ryder said you were an old-fashioned good old boy. I didn't get the difference between a redneck and a good old boy. Northern girl. Yankee, that's me. I Googled it to find out. A good old boy is a person with a strong loyalty to family. And friends."

Marlon was a predator moving within striking distance of its victim. Dirk had seen that heavy stare when they were in the office sometimes. Nothing good came from that reaction.

He leaned down so only she could hear him over the pulse of the music. "Let it go, Alanna. Please. For me."

"I don't want to," she said.

"Please."

He had worked with Marlon. She hadn't. She was

setting herself up for trouble, and they would all be the poorer for it. He had been in many no-win scenarios, and she was about to encounter one.

"Interesting choice of friends you got there, Dirk."

He stiffened and glared at his former co-worker. They'd been friends once, but those days were long over. Now he was the enemy. "Not your business."

She faced him, puzzlement creasing her brow. He nodded to Marlon and almost dragged her down the aisle. She went, but her body was unyielding. He tipped his hat to the doorman as they went past the line of patrons and into the night.

Once they got into the car, Dirk glance at Ally, who met his gaze with a puzzled air.

"Dirk, what was that about?"

He eased the pickup out of the crowded parking area and onto the street. He said nothing until they'd gotten onto quieter streets away from the press of the city. Then he spoke, trying to keep his tone even while fury growled inside him. "Don't you get it?"

"No. Clearly, I don't." She shook her head and then turned her attention out the window. "I was trying to defend you, but you dragged me away like you were embarrassed to be seen with me."

All of his explanations died on his lips. The fury he had been about to unleash on her about her insanity in making it clear to Marlon that they were involved exited his brain when he understood that she had put a different meaning into what had happened than he intended. "Alanna, that's not…damn it."

He couldn't see her face, just the back of her head, but that was enough. He hadn't been married for twelve years without being aware of when a woman was spoiling for a fight.

She said nothing more, and he tossed his hat in the back seat before raking his hand through his hair. The words he sought to say—the ones she deserved—couldn't be spoken. He had no business continuing with this insanity.

"Don't you get it?"

She shook her head, further deepening his impression of her upset. He turned onto a canyon road out of habit, heading toward Alanna's house. He wasn't sure he would be welcome, but he'd deal with that in a minute.

"No. I guess I don't." Her voice was reluctant, as though she hadn't intended to speak.

He ground his teeth, his lips thinning to a mere line. "Alanna…" He again wondered how she could be that naïve. Giving up the fight to sugarcoat his words, he just blurted them out. "You don't know Marlon. I do. When everything happened at Earthy Cry, he led the charge to get rid of me. He went from friend and business associate to enemy. Marlon is the vindictive sort. Y'all put yourself in his sights and tucked his finger on the trigger."

She turned to face him, and her eyes were shadowed with pain before understanding crossed her face. "You're saying… Oh wow, I didn't even think of that. I just saw red."

He controlled his breathing, wanting to pound the steering wheel and ask how she could be so foolish. Yelling at her wouldn't do any good. "You should. We've been careless, Alanna. You don't report to me, so I don't think we're breaking any HR rules, but the appearance isn't good."

"Are you saying..." She gulped in a breath, the pain returning. "Do you think we should stop dating each other?"

The dozens of reasons he should say yes to that question filled his mind. Life would be so much simpler if he did.

"Naw, not that. I think we need to watch ourselves. Like we do in the office. We got to be careful in public too. I can't put you at risk."

She laid her hand over his, and the touch of her skin shot a thrill through him.

"Thanks. I promise. Let's go home."

His relief at the unspoken invitation seared through his nerve endings, shattering Dirk into a million pieces.

Chapter Seventeen

Dirk paused and then threw the pickup into park. Ally waited, unsure of what to say—of what she had done wrong.

"Can I come in? I don't want to end the night like that."

She was glad the darkness of her suburban street shadowed her face, concealing whatever expression she may have had. "I'd like that." She didn't know what else to say.

Something bad had happened at the Whammy Bar. It didn't matter—not right now, with Dirk there in all his glory. She longed to hold on to him and never let him go. When they got to the door, he tugged her inside, kissing her even as she closed the front door.

"C'mon." He linked their hands and led her into the living room. "Forget what happened. You are gorgeous. I've been dying to eat you up for hours." He paused. "I want you so much."

While it might not be a declaration of love, it didn't suck either. "I want you too. Take off your hat and stay a while."

He grunted and did as she suggested, tossing the hat with a flourish. It sailed across the room, landing with a soft whoosh on the living-room floor.

Picking her up, he held her like a groom would hold a bride—and she wasn't going to go down that

197

road. She slung her arms around his neck and pressed into his body.

"I need you like fire." He moved toward the bedroom, kissing her every few steps. Once there, he deposited her on the bed and yanked off his shirt before moving alongside her. She turned on the nightstand light, bathing them in its faint illumination.

He shifted so that she was lying across him, supporting her weight. How did he always know just how much bigger he was and compensate for it in the subtle adjustment of his body?

Frankenstein, without the bolts. A sudden memory of his comment that day at the studio ran through her mind.

"Dirk." Ally had tears in her eyes from the remembrance that this man always felt outsized and loving him for it at the same time. "Would you kiss me again, please? I don't think I can go another minute without your touch."

He urged her up along his body until their lips could meet.

She exhaled against him as his mouth fitted to hers, tongue skimming the inside of her lips before probing deeper. She twisted against him, his powerful frame under her body. When he would have moved to flip their positions, she stopped him.

"Dirk?" she asked again, uncertainty in her voice. "Would you mind very much if I explored you?"

His big hands trembled and eased down her body until they curved around the indentation of her waist. "My body is yours." He kissed her between the words. He loosened his hold on her.

Ally straddled him, knees to either side of his hips.

"I love the way you feel," she said, running her hands across his broad chest before tugging the shirt from the waistband of his jeans. The hem separated from the denim, and she caught a glimpse of tanned skin. She eased her fingers under the cloth and slid it up his body, bunching it as she went. Bending down, she kissed the expanse of hair and muscle she was revealing with light touches of her tongue even as she pushed the shirt farther up. When she reached his shoulders, he took the cloth from her.

With a single, powerful movement, he stripped it off himself and flung it aside where it draped across the corner of her bureau. His gaze never left hers as she raked her nails over the chest she had unveiled, scoring indentations across his pectorals.

His indrawn breath told her that his nipples might be sensitive as well.

"I love the way you smell. I adore your body, your skin, the way you always taste like a combination of rugged man and good, clean earth." She bent down and flicked her tongue across one.

He groaned, a husky elemental sound, his hands on her shoulders, flexing his fingers on her neck.

A laugh bubbled in the back of her throat at the noise, and she turned her attention to the other nipple.

"You like that too." She tasted the curve of his pectorals, tracing the line with her tongue.

"God, yes."

"Good. I love when you shudder." His outrush of breath scorched her, and she leaned in to kiss him, running her hands over his shoulders before her lips touched his.

His mouth opened under hers, his tongue flashing

out to taste her. He lifted the heavy mass of her hair away from her neck and placed a kiss against the frantic beat of her pulse. "Alanna." He moved to switch positions.

"All of you, Dirk." She shifted away from his hands. "I want you to come apart by my touch. Let me." She had to show him how much one person, at least, loved him as he was.

"Darlin'." He arched his back to signal his willingness.

She took the gift, once again kissing the hard muscles of his chest before she moved lower, her nails teasing his nipples before kissing and touching the tensile strength of his flat abdomen, her tongue outlining the line of his hair.

His hips undulated under her as she glided over his skin before settling along his inner thighs, urging his legs apart. She traced the length of him, and he jerked.

A ragged, tearing sound escaped him as her hand played over him. He held her while his body writhed at her touch.

She released the buckle, snaked the belt out of the jeans, and pushed his zipper down over his swollen length. Stripping his jeans and underwear off him, she shoved them down with impatience, letting out a growl when they got tangled with his boots. He reached down and yanked them off his feet where they fell to the floor with a thud.

He was naked, that potent body hers for the touching. She flicked her tongue over the tip of him, and he shuddered. Her hands went to his inner thighs, raking the sensitive flesh there with her nails as she ran her tongue down the underside, tracing the blood vessels there. She skimmed over him until he cried out her name. His fingers curled on her shoulders while she tasted him once, twice, again.

"Please." The word was ragged. "Oh God, please. I want to be inside you. Now."

A flash of a recent fantasy came to her. Her on top, head thrown back, taking all of him. Now.

"Please."

She slid her mouth free of him and glanced up. His face was almost unrecognizable with the desire driving it. His voice had that feral quality, and the thrill it gave her raced through her body like lightning.

"Okay." She stood and stripped off her top and bra, then pulled off her pants while also kicking her sneakers free. She gloried in the moans of pleasure from his throat as her body was revealed to him.

"You're so goddamn beautiful."

"You make me feel that way." After rolling protection on him, she positioned herself above his arousal.

He watched with half-lidded eyes as she took him inside her, all the way down until their bodies met. Big hands gripped her hips, holding her still. "Let me just remember you," he ground out, his baritone a hard rumble.

"Dirk." Her attention was riveted to the sparkling gleam in his eye. She moved against him, and he released her. She swayed over him. The movement made her breasts swing, and he caught them.

"Incredible," he murmured while he was pushing them together until the nipples lay close. With a swift turn of his head, he lashed his tongue across her breasts, catching both in one smooth stroke.

She was caught on something so fundamental there were no words. His tongue, his teeth, his hands, they all combined to make her writhe. She would beg if she had words, but she didn't. She howled her primitive need into the night.

When he caressed her one last time and took her to a basic release, that was all she could do. Scream. Scream his name as everything shattered, pounding down upon his body as an elemental craving came over her. Scream as he drove within her, and then he was shouting her name too. It took her at the same time as the shudder of his release, everything else vaporizing in the world around them.

"Jesus, Alanna," he said when they were through.

She had no words for what they'd just experienced. She sank down to his chest, and Dirk wrapped his arms around her.

"You're Southern and all, but my mother would say Jesus had nothing to do with it," Ally teased, her head resting on his chest with its still-slamming heartbeat, reveling in the heaving of his body. A sudden lassitude started to take her as her fulfilled state overcame her.

Tell him.

She didn't realize she was murmuring under her breath. "Maybe tomorrow I can…"

She fell asleep with the words on her lips.

****

One week passed. Then another.

Something was coming, and Dirk knew it with every instinct in his body. It reminded him of his final days at Earthy Cry when the whispering campaign had started but before they'd amassed enough bullshit to fire him.

This was like that. He was as powerless to stop it as he had been when they found a reason to get rid of him. The difference was more than his ass was on the line.

This time it involved an innocent woman.

He was as boxed in as a steer in a corral. If he preemptively called Marlon to ask him not to punish Alanna, it would inflame things. They might not be breaking the rules—he'd checked that following Monday to be sure—but it didn't pass the smell test.

He should never have let it get this far.

Jess had gone on her opening-act tour with the new consultant, Kai Halara, in tow. Kai was Alanna's friend Terri's old boss, but he was an enigma, saying little as he went about his daily routine. Even before he left, Dirk had discovered very little to latch on to the man but had heard that he was good at his job.

That was good enough. Kai being on board took some of the pressure off Dirk. And Alanna.

Time passed with no word from Marlon. Dirk decided maybe he had been wrong. The man was vindictive, but perhaps this rumor—because that's all it really was—might serve him no purpose.

A body could hope.

In the meantime, he focused on Jess' release. The tour should give her a bounce, but the attendance wasn't turning out the way he'd hoped. He wondered if Marlon had a hand in the situation. The man could have made calls and hampered their efforts.

Or he'd lost his touch. Or they needed to wait longer, try harder. The music industry wasn't as much one-and-out anymore, not in this day of unexpected hits. Jess might get a second album and no more if this first one didn't break.

"Hey, Dirk, you got a minute?"

His stomach clenched as Gordon walked through his open door. This wasn't something he could cure by fighting, and words were what had gotten them here. He wasn't doing a good job keeping this from Alanna, and that was all he cared about.

How had they gotten here?

Alanna was also on the tour with Jess. Then she would be back, and they would have to figure things out. The time for having a discussion was long overdue. He had no words to start the conversation. The ones she deserved—*I love you, stay with me*—were futile. They were too different. He had no business involving her in his world.

Even if he was afraid that was exactly what was on his mind.

"What's up, Gordon?" Dirk wanted to put his hat back on, but he'd learned that Southern California men didn't tend to wear hats—at least not cowboy hats—in a business environment. Here ball caps were more the norm, along with the current fashionable haircut. He hadn't been wrong about the streak of superficiality that ran through this town, but it didn't apply to everyone.

"We need to boost Jess' chart numbers. What have you come up with?"

"I'm working on it. Got her social media fired up, and we're going local to attempt to move the needle. Thanks for your input."

Gordon had taken out ads in each city. Dirk was trying to get an "organic" groundswell going to get the song more airtime.

He loved the marketing part of it—coming up with innovative campaigns and thinking big picture—but the day-to-day grind of the small stuff got tiresome.

"All right, all right, all right." Gordon strode over to Dirk's whiteboard and checked out his ideas. He nodded, but his stiff posture made Dirk uneasy.

"When Ally gets back, we should have a sit-down. We need to course correct this before the album flatlines and her rep goes in the toilet. When is she back?"

"Tomorrow. She'll be done in Vegas. Kai will handle the rest." Dirk said it without thinking and then mentally bit his tongue. Just because he was counting the hours until she returned didn't mean he should be aware of her travel schedule. It had been careless. In this uncertain time period, the smart thing to do would be to act aloof.

"Got it."

He couldn't tell if Gordon noticed or not, but whether he did or he didn't, this could not continue. Something had to change.

"I'll set up a meeting for Monday. Until then, keep working on your ideas. There's some good stuff here." He gestured to the whiteboard and then was gone.

Damn it. He needed something to do. He could go for a run, but that was too citified. On these streets that were nothing but car fumes and traffic. That wasn't going to work for him. Not tonight.

His mind went to that honky-tonk where he'd met Alanna that first night. What was the name of the place? He couldn't recall.

It might do him good to get out of the city and to a place where they two-stepped like they did back home, even if it bore little resemblance to the places back home.

Dirk picked up his hat and began searching the directory for the country bar.

Chapter Eighteen

The burr of the cell phone rang. After ten rings and no answer, Ally pressed the off button and frowned.

Damn. She'd gotten home early in the hopes of paying Dirk a surprise visit, and he was MIA. He rarely went anywhere and had made few, if any, friends in the months he'd been in Los Angeles. She had no clue where he had gone. A small tendril of fear curled inside her before she dismissed it. Dirk wasn't like Harris or Connor. If he was interested in another woman, he would tell her first. He'd do the honorable thing and break it off. That was Dirk, down to his core. Honorable.

She flipped the living-room light on, bathing the room in a soft glow. Her travel bag lay next to the couch. She should have been tired after her whirlwind trip, but she burned with a desire to be with Dirk. The man she loved. All she wanted to do was go to him and put her arms around him, just to feel his body against hers. She'd thought about it the entire time she'd been away. It clung to her like a talisman—but he wasn't around.

She should confide in someone. Terri. Now that her friend had reconciled with Clarke—Ally wasn't clear on the details of how that had happened—she would be eager to hear about others in love.

No. She couldn't do that. If she did tell her old

friend and Dirk didn't feel the same way, she'd have too much to explain. If her house of cards came down around her and he didn't love her in return, then she had to walk away. Having a friend to explain it to might be too much. She didn't have the strength for that action yet. If she kept it to herself, then she would be the only one mourning the loss. She'd be smart to keep it inside so she could swallow the bitter pill and nobody would be the wiser.

She picked up the travel bag and carried it into her bedroom, punching Dirk's cell phone number again. She guessed he was out somewhere, although she couldn't imagine where. She wasn't expected until tomorrow.

Jess was doing okay but not great. The single was placing high in awareness, and it did well with test audiences. She couldn't break through. Ally needed to figure it out—her job might depend on it. Still, they were making progress. Fans were singing along to "Susan" in a handful of places. She spotted some Susan T-shirts in the crowd, and the merch table got more business with each stop. They were making progress but not enough.

Dirk had called her with updates on Jess. Her numbers were flat, which wasn't good. They had a lot of work ahead of them.

Ally threw her dirty clothes into the hamper and put the travel bag away before trying Dirk one last time. Still nothing. She frowned. That wasn't like him. He hadn't cultivated friends in the town. Even the ones from work, or Paige and Craig, were passing acquaintances, reinforced by their mutual relationship with her.

He had not made an effort to fit in—an additional nail in the coffin of her hopes and dreams. If he had it in his mind to stay, he would have found a way. He was stubborn that way.

She sighed and went into the bedroom to play with the cats. They needed her in a way that Dirk never would. Even they were transient. She'd already put in the application to keep the mom and her little black-and-white rascal, but the rest were going to new homes. As predicted, it hadn't taken long for them to get placed. People liked new, shiny things, and baby kittens fit the bill.

She spent a half hour with them and then shut the door to forage some food, smiling when Patches started meowing behind the door.

"Just a little more time," she promised him. "Soon you and Ladymama will have the run of the house."

She debated ordering something bad for her, but she'd had enough of that over the last week. Her pickings were slim. She sorted through her frozen items before selecting some leftover panang from a recipe she'd made. Dirk hadn't liked it, but that shouldn't have surprised her.

She hadn't checked her email in hours. She booted up her computer and surfed her social media, checking on Jess' latest and then switching over to email.

To her surprise a sweet message from Dirk waited in her inbox, telling her he couldn't wait to see her tomorrow. Tonight, he was going to check out that place they'd met the first night. The Horseshoe Saloon. Maybe they could go together sometime. She still had a two-step to learn.

She was tired. She'd been on the road for a week,

and all that had been going through her mind was her sheets and sweet dreamland. Now she no longer wanted to relax.

She gulped down the rest of the meal and darted for the bathroom.

Dirk had a surprise in store for him. He'd said he would teach her to dance, after all.

The Horseshoe Saloon was packed on a Saturday night. Several men milled around the pool table. The bar was standing room only. A band was playing on stage by the name of Travis Miller and his Hometown Bunch, judging from the banner pinned to the back wall. They were a four-piece, with a personable lead singer who had a ready smile for the patrons and a solid tenor voice.

Spotting Dirk, Ally breathed out a sigh of relief. He hadn't changed his mind.

He was on the dance floor, two-stepping with an unfamiliar woman. Ally started toward him and stopped. She had rarely been able to observe him without him being aware. She crossed the room to the pool table and wedged herself into a corner, watching his tall frame.

The couples were wheeling around the floor, whether face-to-face, side by side, or stepping in careful motions. She watched Dirk promenade the older woman, their feet moving together, bodies a comfortable distance apart. His hair was down, covered by a brown Stetson. Boots and a white T-shirt, coupled with Wranglers, completed the outfit.

The two-step ended, and Dirk bowed to the woman and kissed her hand. Then he walked her to a man about her age, presumably her husband. Behind him the band checked their tuning, then the lead singer named a line dance. Dirk returned to the dance floor.

Somebody nearby called the dance the "Tush Push." It consisted of some not-very-complicated moves, ending in a quarter turn and a loud stomp of boots. A middle part required the participants to move their hips back and forth, an action that the graceful Dirk executed so well Ally didn't understand how the women in the room could breathe.

She tried to gauge the patron's reaction to the giant in their midst. To her relief, Dirk attracted attention, but in this type of neighborhood bar, everyone was welcome. He fit in, all six-feet-five cowboy of him.

The line dance ended, and she found she couldn't bear to be away from him for one more second. Watching him was fine, but she'd come here to be with him. She darted toward him, eager for his touch. She hoped he would be glad to see her. She slowed. Would he think she was weird to come? Maybe he wanted to be by himself tonight. Just because he'd told her where he was going didn't mean she was invited.

Can't you see I'm busy? You've got no place here.

She had to get rid of Connor's voice in her head. The man, and his disapproval, were in her past. His power over her was only what was left over from a time when she'd ceded her control to someone else. She wasn't that woman anymore.

She hoped.

He was turned away from the bar, at the edge of the floor. Ally put her hand on his broad back before the band started another song. Dirk pivoted with a social grin on his face.

His face transformed into pure delight when he saw

her. Even she couldn't mistake the emotion. Her heart stuttered, her mouth going dry.

"Alanna."

His baritone held so much warmth that she was glad she had come home early. Lifting her up off the ground, he pressed her to him, his large arms wrapped around her torso as he held her close. Stealing her arms around his neck, she combed her fingers through the silken softness of his hair.

"I didn't expect you until tomorrow."

"They didn't need me. I got out of there, rented a car, and drove back. I tried your cell."

He set her down, his embrace still tight around her. "It's in the car. Didn't think anyone would be calling."

"I didn't think I would either. I surprised both of us."

"I'm glad you did." He gave her a brief kiss, his goatee brushing her skin.

Behind them the band called out a ten-step and started off with a fast beat.

"I couldn't stay in that godforsaken place tonight. You got my email. I didn't think you'd get it till tomorrow. You must be tired, though. You should have rested."

"I did and I am. I couldn't wait. I can sleep any time."

His breath sighed over hers, and he captured her mouth again. "I'm glad." He was silent a moment. "So glad. Time was when I was alone and so lonely the pain drove me to my knees. This week I was alone and lonely, missing you, but you were coming back to me, and that made it bearable. You're my private ray of sunshine."

She longed to tell him the sunshine was his for the asking, for forever and a day. She couldn't. Not yet. Happiness still didn't mean love. Instead, she gestured to the dance floor where the ten-step was ending. "Teach me how to two-step, cowboy. You promised."

"That I did."

****

Dirk took her onto the floor as the next song began and held out his hand to her. Alanna placed her hand in his and looked down at her feet and the boots of the other patrons, shuffling to mimic their placements. Her body hummed with tension against his hands. Her gaze darted around the club like a living thing, reinforcing his notion. He waited, his mouth twitching with the desire to tell her to relax, but no woman liked to hear that. That sort of word ranked right up there with telling them they were being hysterical and other words that a husband learned he did not say to his wife.

Wife. Husband and wife. The image soared through him, and his jaw clenched at the thought.

She stumbled as they began and muttered something under her breath. He kept her moving, guiding her as she fought against the beat, her feet a half a beat behind the dance.

"That's it, you've got it," he said. "Slow…slow…quick, quick." He counted it out for her as Alanna struggled with the move, her gaze toward the ground.

"Stop watching my feet and relax," he said. "You have natural rhythm. Become one with the music."

He searched for a way to tell this woman all the ways that she was better than her mental image of herself, but could think of one sure-fire way that those

213

words made sense. Words he couldn't say. Not now—maybe not ever.

She met his eyes. "It's not a beat I'm used to. I grew up with one-two-three-four. I'm a whiz on the rock dance floor. This is strange. I keep waiting for the downbeat."

"You're doin' fine." He was holding her much closer than he'd held his previous dance partner, his arm around her waist. He fought to keep from hauling her to him and kissing her right there on the dance floor. That wasn't for anyone but the two of them. It would be folly.

Continuing to count the pace out for her, he steered her toward the middle of the floor so the dancers could flow around them.

"I'm no good at this. You should just give up on me and call it a day. It's too formal, and I'm too stiff to make it work. You've probably been dancing since you were a baby."

"Not quite that long. Mama gave us lessons in the barn when I was a toddler." He tried to will her to relax. She could learn this with time. "It just takes practice, and you've got a partner to get it done. I saw you on the floor at the Whammy Bar. You've got everything you need to get it done. Y'all have to trust yourself. You're good at far more than you know."

"If you say so."

His fists clenched against all the things screaming in his mind. If this were two years ago, or if they'd been somewhere he could make a home in, it would all be different. That was a fool's wish. All he could do was play the hand he'd been given. It might be all deuces, and he might be rolling snake eyes, but he couldn't help that.

He kept whispering the dance, waiting for that time when she got it instinctively. Music and dancing were part of who he was, and that same ability lurked inside Alanna. Whoever had made her feel less than—and he had a pretty good idea he knew who that was—he'd love to rearrange their face. This woman was all a man could ask for.

Without warning she found the beat, falling in step with her partner, her body relaxing to the tempo. The beam she turned on Dirk was so radiant he blinked. She shone, the magnetism pouring off her in waves, the infectious grin mesmerizing.

"My God." He slid his arm around her and guided her off the dance floor, his knees shaking in a primal response. "Is that what you used to do? The picture was one thing, but the living woman is something else. I'm surprised the guys didn't fight each other for the privilege of kissing you."

When the song ended, he perched her on his barstool and hovered over her. "You did fine, darlin.' We'll keep practicing, and you'll get better every time."

"I'll get back to you on that. Teach me to line dance too?"

"It would be my pleasure." He pointed to a flyer stapled on the pillar next to them. "Looks like they give lessons if you'd rather do that. If not, we can start with the Electric Slide. Anyone can do that."

"You say that now, but you don't know me. No lessons. I'd rather you taught me."

He waggled his finger in front of her. "I do know you, darlin'. You are capable of far more than that lyin' mind of yours lets you think. It's you who doesn't trust what's right in front of you. You're the one who has to believe, not me."

A man in his early forties with brown hair, Wranglers, and a handkerchief tucked into his back pocket approached, introduced himself as Brian, and asked her to dance.

Dirk took his hat off his head and bowed to the man. "No offense, partner, but my woman here just got back into town, and letting her out of my sight isn't an option. Next time."

Brian nodded and took off his hat in a salute to Dirk. The two men shook hands, and the stranger headed off, pausing by the next table. As the next song started, he led a woman onto the floor, and it filled again with people standing side by side.

She gazed at the dance floor and back to Dirk.

"It's a ten-step. It's a couple's dance, or a pair dance might be a better way to put it, but you're not dancing as a couple." He gestured to the floor, but she shook her head.

"How do you know what's what? To dance to, I mean?"

He shrugged, his attention diverted by the rounded tops of her breasts. Desire stirred, reminding him it had been too many days since he'd been able to touch her as he wanted to. "You learn. Some mix it up and can be both."

He had come here for company and dancing. Now all he wanted was to be alone. With Alanna.

"Whew. That's hard to imagine, but I haven't been doing this since I was a kid. It's fun. Sort of. Once I learn some of the moves, I think I'll enjoy it."

"I'll teach you." He hoped like hell he didn't have

to back out of that promise. This woman deserved to be shown with every move, every breath, how special she was. He was not the man to do that. He was the only man who would do it.

He motioned to the exit, placing his hand in hers. "I can think of a thousand things to do to you, but none of them need an audience. Let's get the hell out of here."

"You got it, big guy."

Chapter Nineteen

Good times, like good food, didn't last. Ally should have known better.

Her first indication of trouble was when Gordon called her to the conference room before she'd turned her computer on. Employees were still trailing in on Monday morning, and this was unusual for Gordon. He wasn't a morning person by nature, and most of his meetings didn't start before ten a.m.

When she got there, Gordon and the employee who also did the HR duties—the ones Ally didn't—sat at the table. A nervous tremor started in her belly. She fought it back, attempting to keep the quaver out of her voice.

"Gordon?"

He waved a hand at her, a gesture that could mean anything.

Dirk entered seconds later, the heavy thump of his boots alerting her to his presence. His frown at the gathered people did nothing to alleviate Ally's panicked nerves.

He met her gaze and then looked away, focusing on Gordon. "What's the meaning of this, hoss?" Dirk spoke in a gravelly tone and remained standing even when Gordon waved him down.

Two folders lay in front of the HR person's hands, and Ally wished with all her might that she could read the contents. Dirk's words from the confrontation with

Marlon rang in her head. *Marlon is the vindictive sort. Y'all put yourself in his sights and his finger on the trigger.*

Gordon studied the doorframe without speaking. After an impatient, silent minute, his assistant came through the door with a folder tucked under her arm. She slid it to Gordon.

Ally's wavering heartbeat quickened.

He glanced at Ally. Then he handed the HR rep the papers.

Ally's fingers came up to twine a lock of hair between them before she caught herself and yanked her hand back down. She was afraid that anything she did would be the wrong thing right now.

"Gordon, I—" Dirk began, but Gordon got to his feet, cutting off whatever Dirk was going to say.

She yearned to bolt up out of her chair, run, and keep running. She'd been doing that for two years, since Connor, and had to stop. Anxiety pounded through her in waves, and she tried to stay focused and not faint. That would also do her no good. She'd played with fire, and she'd just gotten burned.

"I got a call about the two of you. It took me some time to put it all together, which is why I didn't act right away. I've been watching you. You've always denied being anything more than friends, but that isn't true, is it?"

Up until now they had been able to dodge questions about their closeness without outright lying. Ally gulped, anxiety swarming her. Maybe they could get away with it. Then she glanced at Dirk to find him watching her, his body very still.

Dirk still said nothing, waiting for her to take the

lead. If she lied to save one or both of their jobs, he'd go along with it. Even if they got through it, things would never be the same between them. He'd had nothing but denials in his life, and she would be one more friend who turned on him.

"No. It's not. We are…more than that."

Dirk exhaled, and she couldn't tell if he was relieved or angry that she admitted the truth. Whatever that truism was.

"Thank you for telling the truth." Gordon exchanged glances with the HR woman, someone Ally had liked before this. She handed something to him.

Ally wished she were closer. She could always read things upside down, but she was too far away to make out what it said. She was very afraid she knew, though. Final check. Termination papers. She had done everything they asked and waited long past the time when she deserved a promotion. Yet she was being given coal instead of diamonds in her stocking because she had dared break the rules. For once in her freaking life.

"I checked the employee manual, folks. She doesn't work for me, so it's not an abuse of power. I didn't coerce her, and nobody's job is on the line. We are consenting adults."

The words sounded too formal in Dirk's mouth. He might have rehearsed them at some point, anticipating this possibility. She wanted to ask him, to shout something, but she didn't dare.

"That may be, and maybe not." Gordon's statement, like Dirk's, was stiff and unnatural.

After everything she'd done for the company, this was her payback. All the things she did, all the extra tasks she took on, and she was being brought down over the fact that she was sleeping with Dirk? Maybe she didn't show the best judgment in picking someone from the office, but heck, where else was she going to find someone?

"Nah, that's bullshit. There ain't a policy. Not one that's written, anyway. What is going on here, Gordon? Man to man. Don't BS us."

Gordon eyed Dirk as though he hadn't expected the man to be so blunt. He had overlooked that side of Dirk's personality.

None of that mattered. Her career was crumbling to dust around her because she hadn't been able to resist the giant Southerner nor keep her big mouth shut around a man who had become his enemy. She would never get promoted now, and if Marlon had it out for her, she'd be lucky to work in the business again. Her heart sank and then fluttered like a trapped bird. She longed to run. She could not.

"Whether we have a formal policy or not, it can't continue." The HR woman spoke for the first time. She took something out of a different folder and again exchanged eye contact with Gordon.

The seconds dragged out, each one thudding like her heart. Ally had no words, no defense against what was happening. All her normal shields and easy lies deserted her when she needed them most.

"We had to make a choice, and..." Gordon gave Ally a meaningful stare, and her heart fell. Their choice was clear. She had lost.

Whatever Gordon was about to say was cut off by a harsh curse word from Dirk. His face was dark with anger, red spots mottling along his cheeks. His lips were reduced to thin lines, and his goatee twitched. "Stop right there. Don't bother continuing with that horse pucky you're about to spin." Dirk shoved back from his chair and got to his feet. "Y'all are not firing Alanna. You'd be insane to do so."

Gordon shrugged. "I can't have both of you here. Someone has to leave, and you have the better track record."

Dirk snorted and then rapped his knuckles on the conference table. "Maybe what really happened is Marlon got to you. I don't care what the truth is. You aren't going to get rid of her. She's been a good employee for years, and you don't deserve her. She's loyal to you—the good Lord only knows why. You will not fire her. You don't have to."

"Dirk…" Ally started to get up too, but he waved her down.

"You don't have to, because I quit."

The last thing Ally saw of Dirk was his back before he slammed the door behind him.

Ally walked out of Gordon's office, not understanding what had happened. Gordon hadn't said she was fired—and Dirk was gone. The HR person had stared at Gordon when he swore after Dirk left.

Ally was still processing what had happened. Gordon had told her to "go home, and we'll sort it out tomorrow." She might not have a job in the morning. Once, it would have mattered. Now it, like her heart, was broken so effectively she wasn't sure anything could repair it.

At another time she would have called Terri, but her returned friend was in the middle of getting ready for both Clarke's art show and her own wedding preparations. Ally's envy for her friend's happiness kept her from the phone. She had no business calling anyone right now.

She knew where she would wind up. Even understanding that wouldn't go well, she didn't have any choice.

The temporary apartments Dirk still lived in had become familiar to her over the last months, and the guard waved her through. She'd tried to get him to find another home, but he'd clung to the too-small place, declaring he couldn't be bothered to apartment hunt.

He was never going to stay, despite all her efforts. This had been inevitable from the start. As her predictable heartbreak was always going to happen. Only the best romantic destruction for Alanna Wilson.

The dark corridor gave little clue to what she faced inside. These generic places had always been as faceless and cookie-cutter to her as their insides were, but now they mocked her with their sameness. Dirk hadn't moved out of here because he had no intention of giving Los Angeles a chance.

Of giving her a chance.

She hesitated and then raised her hand, rapping on the door before she could change her mind. No doubt he had recognized her tread on the high-traffic rug but made no effort to come to the door. If he wanted her to chase after him, wouldn't he have answered without being prompted?

Too many questions, and they all led to one inescapable conclusion.

For several moments she didn't think he was going to let her in. Or perhaps he wasn't there. She should have checked if his pickup was there.

Then his heavy tread moved on the floorboards, and she held her breath. He was coming. She schooled her face to reveal nothing except bland interest even while her insides were roiling.

His tread stopped, but he didn't open the door. Maybe even now he would turn away and not answer. He would leave her standing there in front of his door like an idiot, grasping for words.

His grim appearance held no surprise when he opened the door to her. He looked down on her from his superior height before widening the door to admit her. His face had no welcome anywhere on it or anything besides a forbidding terseness.

"Figured you would come," he said when she stopped just inside the door. He closed it behind himself, leaving them alone.

Twenty-four hours ago, she would have put her arms around him for a kiss. Now she had no intention of doing so. Not with that grim set to his face.

"I guess I'm that predictable. I needed to make sure you were okay. That was some scene back there." She gestured toward the office building, unsure if she was pointing in the right direction.

"I'm fine. I sent Gordon my resignation ten minutes ago, so it's official. I'm out of Shatter Sound. Unemployed."

"You…" She rubbed her hands together and then on her skirt. The sleek A-line had been a good idea this morning. Now she wished she had something she could run in. Could hide in. "You didn't have to do that."

"The hell I didn't." He moved past her, his head turned away. His things were already taken out from the drawers and stacked on top of the furniture. "You weren't going to take the fall. Not when I was there to stop it."

"We both were responsible for what happened." She longed to shout at him to quit moving but didn't dare.

Dirk collected things from the kitchenette and placed them on the coffee table. She recognized one of them as a mug he'd bought as a souvenir from a gift shop in Angeles Crest. The California state seal now mocked her with its significance where it had been endearing a short time ago.

Her life was crumbling around her, and she was helpless to catch the remnants.

"You were the one with everything to lose. I had no business doing what I did."

He regretted it. The recognition made the bottom fall out of her stomach. She yearned to cry but kept her face still. At the end of all things, she would show dignity.

"I still don't know where all this is going to end up. Gordon didn't say. He may fire me, even though you quit. He was getting ready to do that, I am pretty sure."

Now he did face her, and the bleak desolation on his face made her heart stutter.

"You listen to me. Don't let this happen for nothing. You go back in there tomorrow, and you tell Gordon that you deserve that promotion. Hold out for it. Hell, I should have done this a long time ago when I understood I'd taken it from you. He never needed me—you were always the one. He appreciates it even if you don't. Trust me. Gordon can't do this without you."

He was so forbidding her earlier self would have quailed. This Alanna had nothing to lose.

"To hell with Gordon. What about us?"

He paused in gathering his few possessions and turned to glance at her from the corner of his eye. His hat was off, and his hair hung loose around his shoulders. The locks slid over his face, putting his eyes in shadow. He had started not to hide his face with every turn of his head, but old habits always reasserted themselves in times of crisis.

"Forget about me, Alanna. I don't belong here. I was an idiot to try and fit into a place that was never going to suit me. More than that, with me gone, Marlon will stop coming at you, and you can get the recognition you deserve."

Tears pricked her from within, but Ally wouldn't give him the satisfaction. She straightened her spine, ticking off every time that she didn't weep as a victory. When she was sure she could control her emotions, she bit her lip and then nodded. "I guess that is one way to put it."

He didn't have any boxes to pack stuff, just the two suitcases he'd come with that now rested in the short hallway leading to the bedroom. They had spent many happy nights on that bed.

All of that was over now.

As it always was going to be.

He might have been about to say something in reply, but then he shook his head and picked up the mug. He studied it before setting it back down. "Promise me you'll not take anything less than your due. I've cleared the way for you."

"Do you think any of this is about me becoming a vice president?" The words were out before she could stop them. She almost clapped her hands over her mouth to halt any further rash statements.

"Why not? You earned it. I'm packing up, and I'll be on the road before morning. Listen…" He faced her, and pain moved behind his dour countenance. His goatee twitched, a muscle moving in the back of his jaw.

"Yes?"

He shook his head but then opened his mouth again. "You're a good woman. Don't settle for anything less than what you deserve in that way either. I…if things had been different…"

They are. Say the words, and I'll come. Say them.

"Thanks. You may be in the minority on that opinion. Judging from my track record." *I can add Dirk Roberts to that spectacular flameout. The most tragic one yet.*

"You're one of a kind. Appreciate your worth."

"Sure, whatever you say. I'll work on that. You're heading back to Nashville?"

"Soon as I can get on the road. Nothing left for me here."

Ouch. That hurt more than she could have imagined. Connor, Harris, the things they had done to her paled in comparison to what Dirk was doing under the guise of chivalry. "What are you going to do when you get there?"

He shook his head. "Unclear. Lay low for a while. I told Gordon I'd take my cues from him on how to handle this. He may not announce it right away, in which case I'll keep up the front until he tells me otherwise. Whatever hurts you the least, although I've lost my right to speak on that score." His body shook like a dog trembling after a bath. "I've still got some favors I can call in. I'll make sure none of this rebounds on you. Much as I can, anyway."

She needed to scream at him, but it would do no good.

She had to exit the efficiency apartment and get on with the business of rebuilding her life.

"Thanks for that." *At least.* "Wish me luck?"

"Alanna…"

His big body twitched, and for a breathless second, she thought that he was going to take her into his arms. His hands came up but then fell back by his sides.

"You don't need luck. You're amazing."

Not amazing enough. Story of my life. "Got it. I guess you're all set." She gestured to the mug resting on the counter. "At least you have a souvenir."

He stared at it and then met her gaze. A tragic thing moved over his features and then was gone. He took the mug and wrapped it in a T-shirt before tucking it in his duffel bag. "Right. At least I have that."

"Okay." Without another word, she fled the efficiency apartments.

She was out the door and down the stairs, then she was in her car, backing out of the driveway and heading for the freeway. Thankfully she wasn't that far from home as her driving was not quite steady. She had to get home before she could allow herself the luxury of falling apart. She drove, the 101 yielding to the 170 to her off-ramp. Tears threatened. *Not yet, please. Just a few more miles.*

Her phone rang. Paige. She must have gotten word that her boss had quit. Ally knew she should answer but could not. Paige hung up without leaving a message, and then Ally's text chimed.

The old Ally, the people-pleaser Ally, would have tried to put aside her anguish and reassure her friend. She had no words for Paige, just as she had no empty promises for herself. Everything was shattered, and whatever happened next was out of her control. She'd call Paige back when she was more in control of herself.

She made it to the main street and then her own. Her lips trembled as she pulled into her driveway, but even then, she didn't give in to her anguish. Not yet, not where someone could see. This was her folly and hers alone. She couldn't bear the idea of someone else seeing her stupidity. Fumbling with the lock that fought her as her slippery hands shook with the key, she somehow made it inside. The tears came then, and she fell to her knees.

After a long while she was spent. Her living room was alien to her, like something out of a bad dream. The whole house belonged to an alternative woman from a different timeline. Well, like it or not, this life was back.

I wasn't enough to keep him here. I never am.

Turning the showerhead to pulse, she stripped and climbed in, letting the water take her. With one arm wrapped around her waist and one bracing her on the cool tile of the shower stall, she stood motionless under the beating drops. Scalding hot water mixed with the salt of her tears as she stood there with the water coursing over her, the spray against her back. Tilting her head back, she let the water play over her head, drenching her hair, further obliterating the flow from inside her.

Drying off, she studied her reflection in the mirror.

She looked every bit as dreadful as she imagined. Her eyes were puffy and her face as pale as a ghost. She couldn't put her work clothes back on. She had to get comfortable before she succumbed to the Black Couch of Calcutta. Going to the closet to pull out a sweatshirt, she froze when she opened the door.

She'd forgotten he had left a shirt behind one of the times he stayed there, discarding it in favor of his white sleeveless undershirt when the weather went from cool in the morning to ninety degrees in the afternoon.

Don't do it, Ally.

The shirt went on her body anyway, falling almost to her knees. *One last time won't hurt.* She caught a faint whiff of the earthy scent of his cologne in the cotton. *One last time.*

She let the images from her mental photo album play out in her head. Memories flooded her. The Horseshoe Saloon. The forest. Making love. Wilbur the pig. Tears ran down her cheeks even while the pictures clicked through her mind until they were a whirl with Dirk's face at the center. Then, with an abrupt shake of her head, she slammed the photo album shut.

Netflix and chill wasn't the same when she was alone, but she turned on the streaming services anyway. The cats emerged from the spare room, and the kitten flung himself onto her leg. She picked him up and placed him on the sofa, sliding next to him. He jumped on her and started kneading her belly. Any other time, she would have laughed. Now she just petted the feline with an absentminded stroke, her focus on the choices before her as she sailed through the streamer's offerings, not seeing any of them.

If she avoided anything to do with country music,

she might not cry again.
    Then again, maybe she would.

Chapter Twenty

Dirk drove, keeping his attention on the road in front of him. Only when he'd gotten out of Arizona and the sun was going down did he allow himself to stop focusing on the drive. He didn't need to think about what he was leaving behind in the West—the sight of the sun setting behind him did that in a way no thoughts could.

If he kept driving, he could make it back in two days. He had nothing else to do anyway. He could sleep in his truck when he needed to. Hell, he'd done that before when he was younger. He might not be that twenty-year-old kid anymore, but a catnap in the driver's seat wouldn't be the worst thing in the world. Discomfort would be a good distraction. Hell, he'd earned it. For what he'd just done to the woman he loved, he deserved to be cramped into a too-small seat.

If he stayed on the road, he wouldn't have to think about the stricken expression on Alanna's face when he hadn't said any of the things she hoped he would say. The things he wanted to say but had enough self-possession to stop the words before he altered both of their lives and not for the better.

She thought she loved him. That's what good-hearted women like Alanna told themselves. Maybe she even did. He wished he could believe that she felt the same way he did—that this was the person who completed him, the one he'd been waiting for. She had a life in Los Angeles and a career to follow, and all he was going to do was hold her back. He had to let her go. He'd made the right call.

Even if his soul screamed inside him, it still didn't matter. He did what he had to do. He'd done the honorable thing. He ignored the internal voice screaming to turn around and go back, to drive to that house of hers with the woman and cats inside it that was his new refuge. His new North Star.

His everything.

Damn it.

Dirk tightened his jaw, his hands clenched on the wheel. His knuckles showed white as he gripped the controls, fighting the urge to pivot back the way he'd come.

He focused on the road, watching the mile markers go by with numbing regularity. Each one took him closer to his destination and farther from his heart. The 10 went through New Mexico before it dipped down toward El Paso and through the vast state of Texas.

The sun had long since set, and the freeway had gone from clogged to empty as the cars vanished, replaced by a handful of long-haul truckers and a few intrepid folks out for whatever reason in the late hour. He considered continuing on, but he'd been driving since noon, and the hour was close to midnight. Time to rest.

He considered laying low in the pickup but thought better of it. A roadside sign suggested a motel up ahead in El Paso where he would stop for some shut eye. In the morning he'd pick up the I-20 and go through Texas and Arkansas before making it to Tennessee. He'd leave as soon as he woke up and get some grub.

The GPS said it would take eighteen hours to get there. That was minus traffic, of course, and he had little doubt he'd hit some as he crossed several states. He would be insane to attempt to drive it all in one shot. What the hell else did he have to do? If he focused on his destination, he might be able to stop thinking about the hollow pain on Alanna's face when she understood he was leaving.

He doubted that anything could drive that image from his mind.

Paige had texted him, and he owed her an answer. She was his assistant, and he'd left her high and dry just like he'd left California behind. Her job might be lost now that he'd walked out on the company and his job. His retreat hadn't been fair to Paige. If Gordon fired her, whether out of spite or his position being eliminated, he'd try to help her land on her feet. He owed her that. He'd figure something out, but right now he didn't know what to say to her any more than he had answers for Alanna.

He kept reminding himself he was doing this for her. He needed to be gone to allow her to blossom. She would see that, eventually. Someday she might even thank him. Perhaps she could forgive him when enough time had passed.

Maybe she would, but he wasn't sure the same was true of himself.

He couldn't continue. His lids were drooping, and his body was screaming from the long hours in the cab. Dirk followed the road signs and checked into the fleabag motel advertised that boasted little more than a bed and a dripping shower. He flopped on the bed and slept for maybe four hours before starting his long drive again. He'd been too tuckered out to focus on what he had thrown away, but as soon as he stirred, he started to remember. Time to hit the road again.

His right leg ached from stepping on the gas—no cruise control for him—but he welcomed the twinges in his body. He needed the pains. They would do what his racing mind couldn't, distract him from the understanding that he was making the biggest mistake he had ever made in his life.

He followed the highways to Tennessee, counting off the road signs documenting his progress. He would drive until he couldn't do it anymore. Each mile put between him and Alanna was a victory. Each state farther got him away from committing folly. He was doing the right thing, despite his own wishes.

Turn around. Go back. It's not too late.

Even if he did give in to his emotions, it would do no good. The problems would still be the same. Marlon would still be out to get him and anyone associated with him. Staying with Alanna just ensured she would be caught in the crossfire. He couldn't do that to her, not after she'd worked so hard to get to where she was. He had been a roadblock, and staying would ensure he'd be worse than that. He'd be a career killer. He was still Dirk Roberts, with a stained reputation. When he only had to consider himself, the gossip was tolerable. He could take care of himself. He didn't need much. When it came to the woman he loved, no amount of antipathy was acceptable.

He would have a life to restart when he got back to Nashville. His empty house was there, just as it had been when he left. In better times he'd bought it and fixed it up as time permitted. Despite the move, he had never rented it out. He'd meant to and could have, given the hot market, but he'd chosen to keep it vacant. Part of him must have known this was always a possibility—maybe even a probability. Now he just had to get back and get the utilities turned on. The rest he would sort out.

He had been coming home the entire time. It had only been a matter of when.

It's not too late. Go to her, you fool. She will understand.

He turned up the radio to rid his mind of the echoing words. Nothing could stop his memories from dancing around Alanna. Everything rushed through him. The way she laughed with him. Her clean, womanly smell. The way she cried out and clutched at him when he made love to her. The one thing that might heal his broken psyche was time and maybe not even that. This was the woman he was waiting for, the one that got in his heart and lodged there. Just because he wouldn't be with her didn't negate that truth. He would go on and live his life, but Alanna would always be there, a mockery of the future that could have, should have, been. Of the woman who would be forever branded on his soul.

Years from now he would still have her face in his mind, would still remember her touch, would still have her name on his lips. Time and distance might separate them, but the truth couldn't be escaped. There would never be another Alanna.

Damn it.

****

Ally stood next to Terri, who was observing the

picture that Clarke had drawn for her. Ally tried not to be so envious that she couldn't be happy for her old pal.

"Now that's love." Ally nudged her friend as she spoke.

Terri's gaze went from the picture to the real-life man talking to his guests. It had been a long time since Ally interacted with Clarke Masters, but in her opinion, he was much improved from the dissipated rock star of prior days. She still wasn't sure how she felt about him and Terri being together, but Terri was happy, and that was all that counted.

Unlike one Alanna Wilson. She smiled at her friend, hoping Terri couldn't see the pain in her eyes. She doubted Terri could. Her friend was so blindingly happy she shone from every pore.

"Who would have believed ten years ago that this would ever happen?" Terri turned her attention back to the painting. "Clarke didn't want to show the picture, but I insisted." Her portrait had a *Not for Sale* sign across it. Terri's face in stylized strokes looked back at them.

When Ally gazed at that painting, she couldn't deny Clarke's love for her friend. Ally might not be sure it would last, but the Clarke Masters of ten years ago would never have painted something that emotional. He'd be more likely to paint a whiskey bottle and a cigarette. Or a scantily clad model with himself watching her undress. That Clarke was not this guy, she hoped.

Considering the disaster of her so-called "love life," she had no business judging anyone. Terri had her man in a way that Ally did not. She found an appropriate glad expression and picked up Terri's hand.

"You're lucky." She sighed, a mixture of envy and pleasure in the breath. Images of Dirk danced through her mind, of all the fantasies she'd had about a future for the two of them. She kept her face neutral, although she was afraid pensiveness showed through before she summoned happy memories and made her face brighten. She had no business being a downer on such a happy day. "Great ring."

The channel set diamond and ruby engagement two piece on Terri's finger sparkled in the art gallery lights, almost matching the beam on Terri's lips. Ally fought off the wave of envy. She wasn't jealous—not because of her engagement. Terri had more than earned this happiness. If she wanted what Terri had, that was for her to know. She would tell Terri but not yet. When things were more settled, and her heart wasn't in pieces at her feet.

"I am." Terri peered behind Ally to the gallery beyond. "I was hoping to meet Dirk, the guy you're not dating."

Ally managed a loud scoff. "Not a chance. Dirk would rather chew his arm off than come to something like this. Besides, it's Sunday. Football is on."

Football had been over for a while, but if Terri was aware of the timing of sports events, she didn't show it. If she'd questioned it, Ally would have made something up about the draft or training camp. Terri nodded in an absent gesture, her focus going back to Clarke even though she was still physically with Ally. Ally was familiar with that kind of distraction. She hoped that when she told Terri the truth, she would understand. They had tragic relationships in common, until now.

Whatever else she'd been about to say was lost

when Terri's mother declared, "Tyris, there you are." Ally melted into the crowd, grateful for the escape. Maintaining her composure was a hard-won thing these days, but she'd found that most tended not to ask about Dirk if she redirected their attention back to their needs. Most people were happy to talk about themselves.

She had a hundred reasons why she hadn't told Terri about Dirk yet. The excuse was that Gordon told her to keep it quiet for reasons clear only to him. Still, Terri wasn't in the business anymore, and as her good friend, she could be trusted with the truth. Yet Ally hadn't shared. Her heartbreak was hers alone.

To the outside world Dirk was doing a special project and working from home. Nobody questioned it since the work was getting done, by her and Paige, who Gordon had kept on for the moment. As usual. Dirk also had not surfaced anywhere, although she was sure he was back in Nashville. Or maybe Georgia. Perhaps he'd gone home to family. That was what people did when they were in crisis, didn't they?

The cost to Gordon had been the coveted vice president slot and a raise that wasn't what she was worth, but she took it anyway. Ally thought about telling Gordon to fuck himself and flouncing off, but then Dirk's sacrifice would have been for nothing. She'd earned the promotion, and she would take it.

Even if it no longer had any interest for her.

It had only been a couple of weeks. If she'd recovered that fast, then it wouldn't have been love. She had been miserable when Harris dumped her and gut wrenched when Connor left, but her sadness had been tinged with a healthy dose of relief. Part of her had always known those men weren't right for her, despite what her emotions were. This time she was afraid it would take a long time before she mended. Maybe, like Terri, she'd still be carrying a torch for Dirk ten years from now.

The difference was that Terri and Clarke had a chance that she and Dirk never had. It had been doomed from the start. They were from two different worlds, and he had no interest in fitting into hers—or allowing her into his. Her treacherous heart had understood that and fallen for him anyway. That was how she rolled. Hopeless relationships were her specialty. Maybe she self-sabotaged. She might want to see a therapist about that.

Jess would be back soon from her tour. Ally needed to concentrate on that. That was part of what she got paid for, especially now that Dirk was gone. All responsibility to pull Jess into the public eye fell to her. Terri's old boss and current consultant, Kai Halara, had some ideas for Jess that Ally was eager to hear. The man was an enigma to Ally, although Terri spoke highly of the outwardly calm, composed man. He was stoic in a different way than Dirk, with a centered quality that she supposed might come from his interest in Eastern religion. Ally didn't know and honestly didn't care. She'd heard some interesting rumors about Kai and Jess while they spent time on the road, but that also didn't matter to her. She would focus on Jess' career. That was all she needed to worry about.

Vice president. It had been maneuvered into place so quietly the office wasn't even aware. Paige knew something had happened, of course, and that might have been what prompted Gordon to find her another position within the company rather than release her.

She'd mentioned to Ally that she heard from Dirk, but Ally didn't ask what was said—and Paige didn't volunteer. Her new position was payment for her silence, likely. Ally was glad her friend hadn't taken the hit when Dirk walked out. She felt responsible since she'd recommended Paige for that slot. Ally hadn't told the truth to Paige any more than she'd told it to Terri. Her foolishness was best left to stay in her treacherous heart. Ally's friend would be fine. She would have tried to find Paige something else if she hadn't, but for once she hadn't needed to rescue a person.

Everyone around her had washed up on friendly shores. Everyone except her.

She had been reluctant to sign the contract committing her to Shatter Sound Records for a year, but she had done it. This was her dream—her former dream, anyway. She had nothing better to do with her time. Might as well get what she had earned, even when she'd lost everything. Her original goal fell into her lap, and she couldn't care less.

She had to get out of this pity pot, or she was going to drown in it. It would only make her bitter and ineffective. She couldn't come this far and lose it because of her attitude. She had earned all of this and would make it work. She had nothing else to do.

Dirk hadn't called, of course. Part of her hoped he would, but she hadn't expected it. His exit had been too emphatic, both within Shatter Sound and at the apartment. Those sorts of last-minute declarations of love only happened in novels and rom-coms. Her life was a tragedy, not a TV movie of the week.

Ally gave it a few days, but when he didn't call or text, she made herself remove his texts and emails from her devices. It killed her to do it, but she also couldn't look at the texts every day. Some were so sweet they made her want to weep, and that wasn't healthy. Her actions were necessary—any psychiatrist or friend would tell her that. If she'd confided in any. She only wished that deleting the messages would stop the memories, but they were burned inside her.

She'd been unable to force herself to get rid of his number. The one concession she made to her mental health was to change the name to *Do Not Answer* in case he phoned. Not that it mattered. He didn't call. The slender hope that she'd held on to that he might change his mind faded with each passing day. She had been told a long time ago she wasn't marriage material, and this was just one more bit of proof. She fought the urge to reach out. Her weak mind told her she could allow for a text to check and make sure he got home okay. Every time her fingers itched to send that message, she distracted herself, whether with the kittens or with work.

Each twenty-four hours where she didn't reach out was a triumph of will, and every one made it a little bit easier.

She would get through this. She had no choice.

Chapter Twenty-One

"Ryder. Hoss. I was fixin' to call you." *Eventually.*

Dirk thumbed the phone to speaker as he continued to work on his bathroom sink. His tools were spread out in an array before him, reminding him he had nothing but time.

"Maybe when the cows came home." Ryder's voice held no rancor and a touch of curiosity. "An interesting rumor made its way to my ears."

Dirk's heart fell. He shouldn't have answered the phone but was tired of speaking to nobody but his family and the clerks at the stores. The announcement about Alanna's promotion had gone out, so he no longer needed to hide. Now he could rebuild his life, one brick at a time, just as he was working on the house while he waited to restart his business.

Facing things head-on was better anyway. "Yeah? You heard that that fucker Gordon gave Alanna what she deserved? Or that Marlon tried to screw us all?"

Ryder chuckled, making Dirk long to slam his fist into something. All the rage from those days bubbled over, and he clenched his fists, glad he was clutching a wrench and not his cell phone.

"I did hear that. I also hear y'all is gone from Shatter Sound. I get any of this wrong?"

"Nope."

Ryder waited, but Dirk said nothing else. He

yanked the faucet out of its holding and started to position the new one. He ignored the voice inside him that said he was doing home improvements as a way not to face his demons. Damn demons anyway.

The line crackled, and he shifted the phone with his elbow. The silence stretched until he relented. "Glad that bastard did the right thing. 'Bout time."

"Agree with you there. What about you?"

"I got a house to work on, but now that that's in the open, I'm going to start my own marketing company. Reckon I got the skills to pimp myself out to the public again. I'm back where I belong. I've got a business plan and folks interested. It may take time, but I've got plenty of that now." *Nothing but time, without my woman.*

Ryder chuckled. "I'm going to be in the home-repair business soon. There's a house outside of Austin I've had my eye on since I was a kid that came on the market. You available to help?"

Dirk took a breath before understanding that Ryder was kidding. "You can do better than me."

"Maybe remodeling, but not marketing. I could use a guy in my camp. Earthy Cry is pathetic in that department now that you're gone. The new guys are pencil pushers without an ounce of creativity. I need someone to take me to the next level. If you hadn't said you were going to do that, I would have tried to convince you. Get your company set up, and you've got yourself your first client."

Dirk whistled. "Marlon will not like that."

"I don't care if he gets madder than a wet hen. You let me worry about Marlon. I reckon you've done enough of that. What do you say? You got room for a client?"

He would be an idiot to say no. Despite that, he hesitated for a second. "If you're fixin' to be a fool, then I'm fixin' to take you up on that."

Ryder chuckled. It sounded like he was in the car, judging from the horns Dirk could hear through the speaker. Dirk wasn't sure where Ryder was at this time. Nashville, Austin, Los Angeles, New York—a musician was a man on the road and always on the go. He thought Ryder was off tour, but he had not kept up on any news related to the companies. Maybe Ryder was going to record a new album. The last one had been two years ago. He could do that in Austin and work on this new house of his.

"You're going in to the studio?"

"Soon."

Ryder's clipped tone made it clear more was going on, but Dirk wasn't about to press him. They were friends but not that kind. Ryder had stood by him twice now. That was worth more than Dirk could express.

"Thanks. I mean it. I won't let you down."

"I know you won't. You're that good." Again, Ryder fell silent, the quiet saying more than words could. "I'm almost at the house. When you're set up, email me the details, and we can work out a contract. Dirk...you should rethink your stance on...other things."

He had no illusions to what Ryder meant. A vision of Alanna naked and embracing him made Dirk stagger, his mind swimming from longing. "I can't do that."

"Then you're an idiot, partner. Life ain't worth a hill of beans if the woman you love isn't with you. Trust me."

Ryder hung up, and Dirk tried to turn his attention to the chore he'd been doing. He couldn't avoid images of Alanna. She was better than he deserved, and yet she had been there until he drove her off. He could have gone to her, told her they could work it out, and asked her to stay. Or come. He couldn't do that to her. She earned everything she'd fought for, and he had no business taking it away from her.

Now he had something else to focus on. He had a company to put together and a career to restart.

Things wouldn't be easy. He'd have to overcome rumors and suspicion and perhaps even Marlon sabotaging him. Although maybe the man had done his worst already. If not, he would have Dirk to answer to. This time, Dirk wouldn't go down without a fight.

Time to finish and get cleaned up. He had an LLC to square away.

He tried to ignore the voice inside him that echoed the words Ryder spoke over and over again, like a mantra.

Life ain't worth a hill of beans if the woman you love isn't with you.

He was a fool.

****

Ally stepped out onto the concrete slab that led to her backyard. She picked up the bucket holding the birdseed and crossed the lanai toward the holder in the tree. Sparrows danced in the poplars in the back of the yard, chirping and whirring, hopping from branch to branch. Larger birds, such as crows and blackbirds, waited on the phone lines above, their black gaze intent on her bird feeder.

Her breath was white in the early morning chill, the

tendrils of the grass under her feet wet with droplets of dew. The soft earth was damp and cold to her bare feet, but she welcomed the bracing sensation.

"I'm here, birdies, don't fret," she said, breaking apart bread as she said it. After the bread was scattered, she poured seed into the feeder, one cup at a time.

"Alanna."

Dirk's voice cut through the air. She whirled around, shocked at the sound of it. The bucket slammed hard against her calves, its plastic edge leaving a red slash on the skin.

He was sitting under the lanai, bare head in his hands, hair caught in its usual ponytail. The intensity of his green gaze was apparent even from across the yard.

The pail dropped with a thud, its contents spilling to the ground.

"How did you get in here? How are you here?" She was conscious of her disheveled hair and her unwashed face. Of the fact that the weeks since he had left had not dulled his impact on her senses. She was glad she was wearing oversized sweats. Anything else would have been a mockery.

"I understand Gordon gave you the gig. 'Bout time."

She stared at him, unable to believe he was there. "He did. You got the announcement? Did you get a lot of fallout?" It had been…how long since he left? She ticked off the days, but her mind couldn't tally them up with Dirk in front of her. The reality of him being there kept sliding through her, knocking her sideways.

"Naw. Everyone in the biz knows it should have been yours. Started my own company. Marketing. Ryder Bingham is my first client. He didn't tell you?"

How could they be talking about such mundane things? She had to go past him to return the bucket to its proper place. That was too much effort. Her vision swam, and she was light-headed in the same way it had been before he left.

"He didn't. I'll give him hell for that next time I talk to him. You might have knocked." She ran her fingers through her hair, attempting to comb the strands into some semblance of normalcy. Her fingers caught at the tangle at the ends, and she yanked through it hard, tendrils giving under her tug.

"I wasn't sure what to say."

"Breaking into my backyard was better?"

That made him grin, a gesture which gave her the strength to cross to the lanai.

He rose to his feet, his body showing in the artificial light of her motion sensors. His hair was unkempt, and she yearned to smooth it back and tuck the errant strands into place. Dark rings bracketed his eyes, the lines more pronounced. Early morning light dappled through the poplars, casting shadows across his body, deepening the effect of weariness.

He grunted, and his lips twitched. "Caught me. Reckon you're right about that. Apologies."

She let out a breath. The birds twittered behind her, disturbed by the fact that the humans were still there.

She waved a hand toward him, a thousand words crowding her mind. None of them were right. "I... That's good about the new company. Smart move."

He took a step toward her and stopped. "That's not why I came."

Something inside her broke. "Then tell me why the hell you are here. For God's sake, Dirk, why are you doing this to me? I just got my shit together."

She was revealing too much. She had wished for weeks that he would do something like this, but now that he was here, all she felt was anger.

"I wasn't going to come back. Ever. 'Cept for business if I had to."

Even though she already knew that, the shaft of pain that went through her almost brought her to her knees. The yard swayed, and she was afraid she was going to faint. Her lids closed around unshed tears, and she looked away so he couldn't make out the hurt there. Then she turned away, biting back a cry. Her pathetic hopes and dreams scattered like flotsam on the water, dancing out of reach.

"Then I repeat, why are you here? You can't do this to me. I deserve better."

She kept her head down but noted he was moving by the shadows on the brick. She backed up a step, shaking her head. He would recognize her state of mind the minute she met his gaze. She had to be spared this final indignity.

"Alanna." He put his hand under her chin and moved her head up, turning her to him. "Look at me."

Her crumpled expression must have been even worse than she imagined. His breath caught on a quick, sharp inrush, and his eyes deepened to a dark green when he took note of her face.

Please don't tell me he feels sorry for me.

She found the courage to meet his gaze. She took several deep breaths, calming the quiver that threatened to burst out of her chest. "You owe me an explanation."

"Guess I do at that. When I left, I told myself I was doing the right thing. I didn't belong in Los Angeles, and you had too much to lose by leaving. I was doing both of us a favor. You needed to put me in the rearview mirror just as I put California in mine. That was what I said the entire trip."

She almost stopped breathing, afraid to believe what his words were implying. "What about now?"

He took her hands. His calluses had thickened. Perhaps he'd been spending these weeks working the land. It suited him. Her cowboy was never going to be anything more than he was, and she loved him all the more for that.

She couldn't—wouldn't—tell him that. Just because he was here didn't mean his motives were related to love.

"Y'all sign a contract with Gordon?"

She frowned at the odd shift in topic. "Sure. Just one year, though. My guess is that he had to keep me, so he put me down for the minimum. That's fine with me, though. I just need the year to establish my new title, and then I'll be on the market too. I have no loyalty to Gordon—he had none to me. It's just good business."

His gaze was so intent she had to glance away. She didn't dare fan that slender hope burrowing in her head.

"I always knew you had a head for that stuff."

"Dirk…" Her composure was fraying. She wouldn't be able to maintain this outer calm for more than a couple of minutes…or seconds.

"Listen, I'm going about this all wrong. Ry gave me some good advice. He said that life ain't worth a hill of beans if you don't have the woman you love with you. He was right about that. It just took me a little time to admit it to myself."

"Ryder…said that?" Her voice was faint. If she went above a whisper, she might start shouting.

"Yup. He was right. I'm sorry. I should never have left. Leaving you tore my soul apart, but I did it for you."

She pushed free of his grip, backing up until she was out from under the cover of the lanai. "The hell you say. You walked away from me—for me? You strolled out of my life without so much as a 'see you, ma'am'—for me?" Her laugh was harsh, and he jerked at the sound. Fury boiled inside her, and she fought the urge to dash to the house and yank the door closed. She had no idea what she would do after that. "Well, fuck you, Dirk. Excuse me if I don't believe you. It sounds like a bunch of chickenshit BS to me."

His lips thinned to a slash, and he heaved out a breath. "Ain't nothing but the truth. I hope you can see your way clear to believing me. It's been hell without you."

Now she started shaking in earnest, her long-held, pent-up emotions making her weak in the knees. "I don't believe you. Not anymore."

"Tell me you don't love me, and I'll go. That's why I didn't knock. I needed to remember the good times for a little while in case you tossed me out. You have every right."

"But?" She couldn't process what was happening.

"I'm hoping you don't. I have a long road ahead of me and not much to offer a woman who's a new vice president. I'm praying you'll ignore that on account of the fact that I love you like nothing else."

All her fantasies slammed into her with the force of a freight train. Ally staggered, and Dirk was there. He hooked his arm around her and kissed her in a desperate, rough kiss, his tongue thrusting inside her mouth.

She leaned into him, putting her arms around him and stroking his back, matching his wild need with the same urgency. "You love me? For real?"

He moved back from her and took a breath, then continued. "I've had it in my heart for a while, but I told myself I had to go." His thumbs stroked her cheeks as he spoke. "I'm in so deep it's scary. I need you so much. I was a fool."

"Yes, you were." She tried to keep her face stern, despite the hope soaring through her. She'd been burned so many times before.

She reached up and laced her fingers with his until their joined hands were against her neck. She should say something, but words jumbled in her mind.

"I figure we can work something out if you love me back. Turns out I have to come to LA part of the time anyway. I have lots of incentive. I got a woman there. Her name is Alanna Wilson, and I happen to be desperately in love with her. I think I loved her from the first minute I was in her company. I am hoping she might love me back."

She let him note the adoration blazing in her and made no effort to hide her naked need for him. "You jerk. Of course I love you."

He let out a relieved sigh. "Then we'll figure it out. You, me, those darned cats of yours. I'll commute, or, heck, I'll live here if I have to. The how of it doesn't matter, only the woman. You."

She was going to burst with all the emotions flooding her. The stunning new reality of her life was as fragile as butterfly wings, as incandescent as soap bubbles. "Oh, Dirk," she cried, moisture trickling down her face. This time, though, they were tears of happiness. "I can't believe you love me."

He pressed a kiss on the inside of each of her palms and then tilted his head up to her again. "That I do. I love you. I love you now, and I'll love you until I die."

She thought of all the things she could say. So many things in their future. Two strong, tall boys, with an appreciation of the earth. A girl with her father's green eyes, confident and capable. Them sitting on the porch, their love steady through the decades, as endless as the land and as deep as the sea. They would grow old together, their commitment unwavering through the years. She would tell him all these things at some point, but she had time. First, he'd posed a question she longed to answer.

"There are no words except these, and I've wanted to say them for so long." She slid her arms around his body and gazed deep into a face that shone back his love. "I love you, Dirk Roberts. From always until forever."

He caught her to him, whispering snippets of the same dreams she'd had—of love, their children, so alike as to be two parts of the same whole. He sighed over her lips until they were embracing as their future coalesced around them.

It didn't matter where they were. In each other's arms, they were home.

A word about the author...

Claire can't remember a time when writing wasn't part of her life. Growing up, she used to write stories with her friends. As a teenager she started out reading fantasy and science fiction, but her diet quickly changed to romance and happily-ever-after. A native of Massachusetts and cold weather, she left all that behind to move to the sun and fun of California, but has always lived no more than twenty miles from the ocean.

In college she studied acting with a minor in creative writing. In hindsight she should have flipped course studies. Before she was published, she sold books on eBay and discovered some of her favorite authors by sampling the goods.

While she's not a movie mogul or actor, she does work in the film industry with her office firmly situated in the 90210 district of Hollywood. Prone to breaking out into song, she is quick on her feet and just as quick with snappy dialogue. In addition to writing, she does animal rescue, reads, and goes to movies. She loves to hear from fans, so feel free to drop her a line.

~*~

Find Claire online at:
http://www.clairedavon.com

Thank you for purchasing
this publication of The Wild Rose Press, Inc.

For questions or more information
contact us at
info@thewildrosepress.com.

The Wild Rose Press, Inc.
www.thewildrosepress.com